J. K. Davis

The Sailor's Companion

Selected and Arranged

J. K. Davis

The Sailor's Companion
Selected and Arranged

ISBN/EAN: 9783337277260

Printed in Europe, USA, Canada, Australia, Japan

Cover: Foto ©Andreas Hilbeck / pixelio.de

More available books at **www.hansebooks.com**

THE

SAILOR'S COMPANION

SELECTED AND ARRANGED

BY

J. K. DAVIS.

CHAPLAIN AT TROY, NEW YORK.

"And thou Solomon, my son, know thou the God of thy father, and serve him with a perfect heart, and with a willing mind; for the Lord searcheth all hearts, and understandeth all the imaginations of the thoughts; if thou seek him he will be found of thee; but if thou forsake him, he will cast thee off forever."—1 CHRONICLES, 28, 9.

NEW YORK:

ROBERT CARTER & BROTHERS,

530 BROADWAY

1864.

STEREOTYPED BY
BILLIN & BRO'S
10 North William-st.

R. CRAIGHEAD,
PRINTER,

CONTENTS

———〰〰〰———

THE SAILOR'S COMPANION.

EXTRACTS FROM PERSUASIVES TO EARLY PIETY,

BY REV. J. G. PIKE.

"My young friend, if a person could rise from the dead to speak to you; could come from the other world to tell you what he had seen there, how attentively would you listen to his discourse, and how much would you be affected by it! Yet a messenger from the dead could not tell you more important things than those to which I now beseech your attention. I come to entreat you to give your heart to God; to follow the divine Saviour *now;* and to walk in the pleasant paths of early piety. O that I could, with all the fervor of a dying man, beseech you to attend to your only great concerns! for of how little consequence is this poor transient world to you, who have an eternal world to mind! It is not to a trifle that I call your attention, but to *your life,* your all. your eternal all, your God, your Saviour, your heaven, your every thing that is worth a thought or a wish. Do not let a stranger be more anxious than yourself for your eternal welfare. If you have been thoughtless hitherto, be serious now. It is time you were so. You have wasted years enough. Think of

1*

Sir Francis Walsingham's words : ' While we laugh all things are serious around us. God is serious, who preserves us; Christ is serious, who shed his blood for us; the Holy Spirit is serious, when he strives with us ; the whole creation is serious in serving God and us; all are serious in another world ; how suitable then is it for man to be seri· ous ! and how can we be gay and trifling ?' "

" Do you smile at this grave address, and say, This is the cant of enthusiasm ? O, think, that those who laughed at these solemn truths when the last hundred years began, now laugh no more ! The friendly warning may be neglected, and the truths of the Bible disbelieved ; but death and eternity will soon force on the most careless heart, a deep conviction, that religion is the one thing needful.

" Yes, my young friend, one thing is needful ; so said the Lord of life ; needful to you, to me, to all. The living neglect it, but the dead know its value. Every saint in heaven feels the worth of religion through partaking of the blessings to which it leads ; and every soul in hell knows its value by its want. It is only on earth that triflers are to be found ; and will you be one of them ? God forbid !

" Reader, I beseech you, read this little book with ·erious prayer. Remember that it is your welfare which is sought. I wish you to be happy here, and when time is past, happy forever. Fain would I persuade you to seek a refuge in the skies, and friends that never fail. I plead with you a more important cause than was ever conducted before an earthly judge. Not one which concerns time only ; but which concerns a long eternity. Not one on which a little wealth or reputation do·

pends; but one ou which eternal poverty or eternal riches, eternal glory or etcrnal shame, a smiling
or a frowning God, an eternal heaven, or an eternal hell, are all depending. And it is your cause
I plead, and not my own; and shall I plead your
cause to yourself in vain?

"I know, my young friend, how apt we are to read
the most serious calls as if they were mere formal
things, of little more consequence to us than the
trifles recorded in a newspaper. But do not thus
read this little book.' Believe me, I am in earnest
with you; and read, I entreat you, what follows, as
a serious message which I have from God for you

" Consider what will be your thoughts of the advice here given you a hundred years hence. Long
before that time, you will have done with this world
forever. Then your now vigorous and youthful
body will be turned to dust, and your name probably forgotten upon earth; yet your immortal soul
will be living in another world, and far more sensible of joy or grief, than it can possibly be now.

" Then, my young friend, you will think of this
friendly warning; how happy you will be if you
have followed the advice it contains! Fancy not
that it will be then forgotten. Calls and mercies
forgotten *here*, must be remembered *there*, when
every sin is brought to the sinner's memory. If
now you think me over-earnest, you will not' then
entertain the same opinion. If now you slight
this humble effort for promoting your salvation,
and carelessly or contemptuously throw this book
aside, if then ten thousand worlds were yours, they
would appear a trifle, for another season of salvation, like that you now enjoy, and which, perhaps,
you now waste. But now is *your* day of grace;
then, another generation will have theirs.

"Think again, that while you are reading this,
thousands are rejoicing in heaven, that they, in
past years, attended to such earnest calls. Once
they were as careless as you may have been, but
divine grace disposed them to listen to the word
of life. They regarded the warnings addressed to
them ; they found salvation ; they are gone to rest ;
and now with what pleasure they may recall the
fervent sermon, or the little book, that under God
first awakened their attention, and first impressed
their hearts ! Think also, that while you are reading these lines, millions of wretched souls, in utter
darkness and despair, are cursing that desperate
madness which led them to turn a deaf ear to such
friendly warnings, once addressed to them. O my
young friend, I beseech you, by the joys of saints
in heaven, and the ten thousand sinners in hell,
trifle no longer with this affectionate call ! Did
we feel the thousandth part of the worth of an immortal soul, I might abhor myself for writing so
coldly ; and you blush and be confounded, at having needed warning to seek its welfare. It is impossible to be earnest enough with you: if you
ever know the worth of true piety, you will be
convinced that it is. Did we see thousands asleep
on the brink of a precipice, and some every moment falling and dying, could we too earnestly endeavor to awaken those not yet undone? O my
young friend, if you have been a careless trifler
with the Gospel of Christ, danger infinitely worse,
eternal danger threatens you ! Awake, awake !
I beseech you, awake before it is too late ! before
eternity seals your doom ! before God forgets to
be gracious ! Awake ! as in the sight of God I
call on you, awake ! close not your eyes to sleep in
sin again ! Lest

You should shortly feel
The sleeper sleeps no more in hell.

Awake! I beseech you, and begin to mind that one thing, which is so needful to you. Perhaps all I urge to gain your attention is urged in vain. And shall it be so? Will you slight your God, and make your own destruction sure? Alas! if you will, what must be your condition soon? But let me hope better of you, and offer you one request: look up to God, in the following prayer, and beg his mercy on your precious and immortal soul.

" Great God, thou seest me, a young and thoughtless creature. Young as I am in years, yet far have I gone in sin. So far that thou mightest justly have said with respect to me, 'Cut down that cumberer of the ground;' and had that dreadful sentence been long ago pronounced and executed, I must have owned it just. My years are few, but my sins are many; more numerous are they than my days or hours;—more countless than the hairs of my head. Alas! blessed God, what a part have I acted! I have received life from thee, and employed it in neglecting and sinning against thee. I might have died at my birth, have seen the light and closed my eyes in death, but thou didst watch over me in infancy, didst guard me in childhood, and hast brought me to the blooming days of youth; and how have I requited thee? Wretch that I have been, to requite thy love with ingratitude, thy goodness with neglect. Distracted creature that I have been, to spend the flower of my years in grieving thee, my best friend; in pleasing Satan, my infernal foe; and in undoing my own immortal soul. O, make

me sensible of my sin ; teach me to bewail and
loathe my folly, and help me to forsake it !· Now
let me begin to live that life, which, on a dying
bed, I shall wish to have lived. Pour out thy
Spirit on me, for he alone can teach me what thou
art. Give me to thy Son, and thy Son to me.
Teach me to regard the truths I read. May the
persuasives and motives here presented to me,
reach my heart, and may I be no longer the
thoughtless creature I have hitherto been ; but
may I chooɟe that good part which shall never be
taken away from me. Teach me what I am, and
lead me to Jesus Christ, thy once crucified, but
now exalted Son. O, make me thine ! O Saviour,
make me thine ! O God of glory, make me thine
without delay, and teach me all thy will ! Then,
whatever be the instrument that awakens my soul,
thine shall be the praise, for it is thy work, and
the glory is justly thine. Hear me, O thou most
merciful Father, and wash my sins away in aton-
ing blood ; hear me, and let my youth from this
day be devoted to thee ; hear me for the sake of
thy beloved Son : and now to Father, Son, and
Holy Ghost, as to the King eternal, immortal, in·
visible, the only wise God, be glory and dominion
world without end. *Amen.*"

THE FALLEN, GUILTY, AND RUINED STATE
OF MAN.

" I now, my young friend, address you on a sub
ject unspeakably important ; as no hope can be
entertained of doing you lasting good, till you feel
the truth of the statement just repeated. In ref·
erence to bodily disorders it is said, that to know

your disease is half the cure. The same observation will apply to the disorders of the soul. If one deeply infected with a fever, or the plague, were so deluded, as to believe himself enjoying perfect health, or to think himself at worst, but slightly disordered, and therefore to neglect the means for restoring health, how soon would death and the grave convince him of his sad mistake! Such delusion is seldom met with; but an infinitely more dreadful delusion is as common as the light of day. Perhaps you labor under its influence. Perhaps, if your life has been unstained by flagrant enormities, you imagine yourself a good-hearted young man. Your sins are softened down under the name of youthful follies. The deep corruption of your nature is totally hidden from your view. You are in danger of dying eternally of the worst of plagues, and yet think that all is well. You are exposed to the wrath of a justly offended God, and saying to yourself, ' Peace, peace.'

"God forbid that I should represent your state, by nature, as worse than he describes it in his word.

"Be patient, then, and hear the worst. What are you? If guided by the opinions of a poor, blind world, you might reply, 'A frail, imperfect creature, guilty of some sins, but yet, with so many good dispositions and good actions to counterbalance them, that I may reasonably hope for happiness and heaven.' My dear young friend, are these, or such as these, your view of yourself? If they be, no wretched madman, bound with chains, crowning himself with straw, and imagining himself a mighty and happy monarch, was ever more deceived. I repeat the question,—What are you?

Let the word of the God of truth reply. And what is its answer? It teaches you that you are corrupt, and polluted, and at variance with God; having all the powers of your soul disordered; and exposed, justly exposed, to everlasting ruin; and so entirely depraved and undone, that without a change as great as a second birth, you cannot possibly see the kingdom of God.

"Perhaps you exclaim, 'Shocking doctrine!' whilst full of indignation, you are almost ready to throw this book aside, before you have looked at the proofs afforded in scripture for these assertions. If this be the case, I beseech you remember I appeal to scripture, not to your passions; to the declarations of God, not to worldly delusions. You may cry out at the sight of a shroud, a coffin, a grave, 'Shocking objects!' but your loudest exclamations will not lessen the awful realities, by which many have happily been shocked into a timely preparation for approaching death.

"The word of God assures us, that every human being is born into this world with a corrupt and sinful nature God formed man 'in his own image,' innocent and holy; but fallen man begat a son 'in his own likeness,' corrupt and fallen, like himself. The consequence is, man comes into this world with a sinful nature; for 'who can bring a clean thing out of an unclean? not one.' Such is the exceeding sinfulness of human nature, that the word of God strongly describes it, by declaring that we are 'shapen in iniquity and conceived in sin. 'Man is a transgressor from the womb, and goes astray speaking lies.' The devil is elsewhere called the father of lies; and one of the earliest tokens of human depravity is, that a disposition to commit that abominable sin so soon appears in little chil dren.—Man is born untamed and rude as a 'wild ass's colt.' 'Foolishness is bound up even in the heart of a child.' 'The imagination of man's heart is evil from his youth,' 'is only evil continually;' 'he is abominable and filthy, and drinketh in iniquity like water.' As he advances in life, do his corruptions weaken? The words of the apostle answer, No: 'We ourselves, also, were sometimes foolish, disobedient, deceived, serving divers lusts and pleasures, living in malice and envy, hateful and hating one another.'"

This sinfulness of our nature, my young friend, is not partial; it is not confined to some of your powers and faculties; but, like a mortal poison, spreads through and pollutes the whole. The heart, which should be the best part of man, is now the worst. "The heart is deceitful above all things, and desperately wicked." Such are the windings of its corruption, that no eye but Jehovah's can trace them out. It is *full* of evil; not merely tainted but filled with sin; and "madness dwells in it." The eyes, the ears, the hands, the feet, the lips, are all defiled by different sins; and the tongue, that member which was formed peculiarly for its Creator's praise, "is now a world of iniquity; and is set on fire of hell."

"Man is not only so extremely sinful that he cannot please God, but so *blind* that he is entirely ignorant of what is acceptable in his Maker's sight. *So awful* is this blindness, that the 'the natural man receiveth not the things of the Spirit of God, for they are foolishness unto him.' Even the 'preaching of the cross itself is to them that perish, foolishness.' And *so wilful*, that 'men love darkness rather than light, because their deeds are evil; and proceeding in their career of madness, 'fools

make a mock at sin.' Is it possible, my young
friend, to give a sadder representation of the nat
ural blindness of the heart than these passages
give? Sin, which God declares to be the cause of
misery, death, and hell, men treat as a matter of
foolish ridicule and mad laughter; while that glo·
rious plan of salvation which so magnifies the wisdom and love of God that it astonishes the angels
of heaven,—even this is folly in view of poor unconverted men. The man who should laugh at a
thousand swords aimed at his defenceless head, or
pointed at his naked breast, were wiser than he who
laughs at sin. Less foolish were the wretch who
should treat as folly, a plan to deliver him from the
condemned cell,*the halter, the gibbet, or the fire,
than he who thus treats the wondrous plan which
God has devised, to save him from the flames of
hell.   ·

"It is written, the 'carnal mind is enmity against
God.' A more awful description of fallen man
cannot be given, than that contained in these few
words. The carnal mind is strictly the earthly
and sensual mind; that which the moral and the
profligate alike possess, while loving the world and
the things of·the world. The miser, as well as the
spendthrift; the pleasing young man that is following earthly objects with all his heart; the en-
gaging young woman whose thoughts are fixed on
fashion, dress, and gayety, as much possess the carnal mind as does the shameless profligate, whose
conduct they abhor; and the sober tradesman,
whose plans and schemes all refer to this world. is
as much under its influence as either of the others.
All these have a worldly or carnal mind, and what
is it? enmity against God,—enmity itself. What
can be worse than this? The Scriptures assert pos·

itively, that this is the condition of all men. 'All have sinned and come short of the glory of God.' This holy book also gives us an affecting account of the danger to which, as a fallen creature. and a sinner, you are exposed. By the God of eternal truth are you assured, that men are 'by nature the children of wrath;' that 'he that believeth not is condemned already;' and that 'judgment has come upon all men to condemnation;' and that men, as sinners, are in a state of death; that 'the wages of sin is death,' and that 'the soul that sinneth, it shall die.'

"And now, my young friend, what are your views of your own state? Do you feel that you are in a lost state, and that the 'wrath of God abideth on you?' Do you feel that nothing but the brittle thread of life separates you from that 'indignation and wrath, tribulation and anguish,' which Almighty God has most solemnly declared he will inflict upon all the transgressors of his law. who die in their sins; or do you disbelieve all this, and say, 'I shall have peace,' all will be well at last Perhaps you may have been an affectionate child, you may be tender and compassionate, dutiful and obliging; but will this save you? No, never; excellent as these qualifications are in their place, if these could have atoned for sin, and saved the soul, the Son of God need not have died. But the fact is, you may possess all these, and yet live in rebellion against God; and thus, however fair your character may be in the sight of men, in that of God it may be as dark and as vile as the character of Satan himself. You see then that you are in a lost state, and that without a change of heart you cannot be saved.

"Shall I be more particular, and specify some

of the sins common to youth ; such as the follow
ing ?—Pride, disobedience to parents, waste of
precious time. Time is given us to prepare for
eternity ; but, alas! how are its golden hours sinned and trifled away! One of the most common
ways, in which time is wasted, is in the employing
of it on romances, plays, and novels. If you are a
novel reader, think the next time you take a novel
into your hands, how shall I answer to my Judge
for the time occupied by this? When he shall
say to me, ' I gave you so many years in yonder
world, to fit you for eternity. Did you converse
with your God in devotion? did you study his
word? did you attend to the duties of life, and
strive to improve to some good end your leisure
hours?' Then, then shall I be willing to reply:
' Lord, my time was otherwise employed! Novels
and romances occupied the leisure of my days ;
when, alas! my Bible, my God, and my soul were
neglected?' "

Sabbath-breaking, although not confined to'
youth, is a very common sin among them. A
Sabbath-breaker is justly described as one who
despises his Maker; rebels against the King of
kings, defies his vengeance, provokes his wrath ;
disgraces the Christian name ; tramples on the
laws of his country ; ruins his own soul; and poi-
sons others by his fatal example.

" Taking pleasure in the sins of others, though
one of the most awful, is one of the most common
of human iniquities; and abounds among none'
more than among the young. The lewd and profane, tempt others to lewdness and profaneness.
The thoughtless and the gay, persuade others to
imitate their levity and their folly. As if it were
not sufficient to have their own sins to account for

many thus make themselves partakers in the sins of others; and, as if it were not enough to ruin their own souls, many thus contract the guilt of assisting to destroy those of their companions and friends. Have you never led others into sin? Perhaps some, who are now lost forever, may be lamenting, in utter darkness and despair, the fatal hour when they became acquainted with you. Have any learned of you to trifle with religion ; to squander away their golden day of grace; to slight their God; and choose perdition? If not by words, yet, perhaps, by a careless and irreligious example, you have taught them these dreadful lessons."

A PRAYER FOR A YOUNG PERSON WHO IS SENSIBLE HE IS IN A SINFUL, DANGEROUS, AND LOST STATE.

" O Lord, my God, thou hast not been in all my thoughts. By my ungodly life, I have said to thee, ' Depart from me, for I desire not the knowledge of thy ways ;' and though thy beloved Son, once crucified for my sins, has claimed my heart, I have refused to listen to his call. And yet I have deceived myself; and have deemed myself almost innocent; have thought my life righteous; and treated humble piety with contempt and scorn. True wisdom I have counted folly, and folly prized for wisdom. · Merciful Lord, my lips, my tongue, my eyes, my ears, my hands, my head, have all sinned against thee : but, oh, my heart! the heart I deemed good, what madness has dwelt there! There have those corruptions abode, which hell takes pleasure in viewing, but which heaven must mourn to see. There anger has burned. There pride has swelled There envy and revenge have

2*

rankled. There vanity, indolence, discontent, ingratitude, and all the detestable brood of human
vices, have shown their hateful forms. And shall
I now plead that I am innocent? Shall I now declare, that my heart is good, and my transgressions
few? Merciful God, forgive the blindness which
deluded me with thoughts like these. No, O my
injured Father, the smallest sin against thee, is
huge as the frowning precipice, dark as the shadow
of death, and horrid as the depths of hell; and the
smallest of my crimes have been as much committed against thee, as the more profligate actions of
some, who never enjoyed the instructions with
which I have been favored. I have lived long
enough; alas, too long! to the world, to Satan,
and myself; now let me live to thee. Now, for
Jesus' sake, guide me from sin to holiness; from
folly to wisdom; from death to life; from vain delight to real joy; and, finally, through the Lamb
that was slain, advance me from earth to heaven,
there to praise, bless, magnify and adore redeeming love, through ages without end. O gracious
Lord, hear my requests, for Jesus' sake. *Amen"*

THE NATURE OF TRUE RELIGION BRIEFLY DESCRIBED.

" That religion is the chief concern of all, is the
declaration of the Most High; and early religion
is what he solemnly requires. 'Remember now
thy Creator in the days of thy youth;' those best
days, prepare to meet thy God. While young
make him your friend; seek an enduring mansion
in the skies, and thus, to every other source of
cheerfulness, add those last and best, your heav-

enly Father's care, and your gracious Saviour's love.

"Most persons will acknowledge the excelleney and importance of religion, yet few are its real friends. 'Few there be that find it.' Many are entirely careless of it. Others have the form, without the power. Others play the hypocrite's part; they 'speak fair words and act foul deeds; lift their eyes to heaven, and turn their steps to hell.' Youthful reader, while I endeavor to describe to you what religion is, let me beseech you to unite your prayers with mine, that you may indeed be taught of God. Let me beseech you to attend as seriously to the plain and affectionate truths that may be presented to you, as you would do if lying on a dying bed, and there earnestly inquiring how salvation may be found.

"Religion consists in such a practical knowledge of our own guilt and misery, as leads us to abhor sin and ourselves; and in such an acquaintance with the blessed God, and the adorable Saviour, as leads us to believe on Jesus for salvation, and resting all our hopes upon his atonement and righteousness, to trust our eternal all to his care, and to yield up ourselves, body, soul, and spirit, to the Father as our Father, to the Son as our Saviour, and to the Holy Spirit as our Sanctifier.

"The foundation of religion is laid in a knowledge of our own guilt and depravity. As sickness teaches the patient to prize the physician's aid, as slavery leads the captive to seek for liberty, and condemnation makes the criminal cry for mercy, so the knowledge of our own condemnation and guilt prepares the soul for the reception of Jesus Christ. Are you acquainted with this? Are you sensible that you have rebelled against a God of

love? and are you penitent for your transgressions?
You cannot else escape destruction. The Lord has
declared, 'Except ye repent, ye shall all likewise
perish.' 'God now commandeth all men everywhere
to repent.' This repentance consists not in a
transient sorrow for sin, but in such a sense of its
evil, vileness, and ingratitude, as begets in the sou.
abhorrence of it, and an anxious desire for deliv·
erance from its power and punishment. If knowledge of yourself, and the evil of sin, has humbled
you in the dust, and led you from the heart to ex·
claim, 'God be merciful to me a sinner!' then,
permit me add, that a most essential part of relig.
ion is an acquaintance with the Lord Jesus Christ.
Not a mere speculative knowledge of his excellen
cies, like that which even an infernal spirit may
possess, but such a practical knowledge of his power
and grace, and such a belief in him, as subdues the
soul, and leads the penitent sinner to make Jesus
his hope, his trust, and his all.

"In the case of man, and in your own case, sin
has deserved eternal punishment. The justice of
God called for the execution of the sentence of
condemnation. But his wisdom devised a plan of
mercy for a rebellious world; and his compassion
induced him to adopt the plan. It was, that his beloved Son should suffer for man, and bear the curse
instead of him   Thus would sin be punished; and
thus might the sinner be *entirely* forgiven. Thus
did God give to his whole intelligent creation an
awful proof that sin, in his dominions, could not
escape unpunished. Yet, while· showing his· infi.
nite hatred of sin, he showed his infinite love for
ruined man, in thus appointing his beloved Son to
stand in the sinner's place, and in thus punishing

in Christ the sins of man, that the penitent sinner might go free.

"An acquaintance with this divine Saviour is absolutely needful for you. He is set forth as the only foundation for the sinner's eternal hopes. 'Believe on the Lord Jesus Christ, and thou shalt be saved.' But, my young friend, permit me affectionately to caution you against deceiving your own soul with the shadow of belief, instead of the substance; for, in one sense, 'the devils believe and tremble.' Believing in Jesus is termed, in Scripture, 'believing with the heart.' There is the consent of the heart to this plan of salvation; as well as the persuasion of the mind. If you truly believe on Christ you will receive him as your Lord, your hope, your Saviour, your all. A well-placed trust in Jesus Christ will be found a sure support for hope, and peace, and joy, when all other dependencies sink in eternal ruin, and all other hopes are blasted in black despair. The soul, committed to his care, will be safe through its little stay among the objects of time and sense; and, what is far more important, will be safe and happy when the graves are giving up their dead, when the world is fleeing from the majesty of its Maker's face, and when creation is perishing in final flames.

"If you, from your heart, receive the Lord Jesus Christ as your Redeemer, you will also submit to him as your sovereign Lord; you will love the commandments of God, as just and holy; you will yield up yourself, body, soul, and spirit, to the Lord Jesus Christ; that whether you 'live, you may live to the Lord; or whether you die, you may die to the Lord.' While religion leads you to trust the Saviour s Death, it will lead you to copy his life.

"Wherever the precious Gospel is embraced, and Jesus followed, a change most truly glorious and divine, will take place. Under its heavenly influence man becomes a 'new creature: old things pass away and all things become new.' Let the passionate come to Jesus; and mildness, in their breast, will take the place of anger. The covetous will grow liberal; the proud, become humble. Drunkards, learn sobriety; and liars love the truth. Thieves become honest. Sabbath-breakers improve the sacred days they wasted once. The prayerless learn to pray, and find their duty and their pleasure united in devotion. The hard-hearted change their natures for compassion. The earthly-minded renounce the things of earth, and seek their treasures in heaven. And they who are addicted to what are commonly esteemed the most incurable vices, under the influence of true religion, change pollution for purity, wickedness for holiness, and the likeness of devils for the likeness of God.

"The Lord Jesus Christ places the value and importance of real piety in a most striking light, in the history of Lazarus and the rich man, Luke xvi. 19, &c. Lazarus is described as poor, despised, afflicted,—a beggar without an earthly friend. He has lived in poverty, and at last, unable any longer to glean his scanty pittance by wandering from door to door, he is laid at the rich man's gate, worn down with sickness. No kind relation, no benevolent friend cheers him. The crumbs which fall from his wealthy neighbor's table are his support. His tattered rags scarcely cover the spreading wounds in his disor-

dered and dying body; the dogs come and lick
his sores. Is it possible to describe more compli-
cated wretchedness? But he dies; and now he
who had not one friend on earth, has angelic
friends to conduct him to the regions of glory.
Now farewell to poverty, to begging, to grief, to
tattered rags, to painful wounds, to earth and all
its sorrows He, who had no abode here, finds an
eternal abode in the mansions of bliss. He, who
was an outcast upon earth, walks the golden
streets of the New Jerusalem, and is become one
of the hosts of saints and angels clothed in light.
Near him, while upon earth, lived one, who enjoyed in abundance the pleasures, gayeties, and
honors of a dying world. But his all was in this
world, he had nothing beyond the grave. At
length he died. The skill of physicians, the tears
of friends, and all the care of attendance which
wealth commands, cannot ward off the stroke of
death. He dies, and lifts up his eyes in hell.
Which was the happy man? Which the possessor of real treasure? Surely you cannot hesitate
to say, Lazarus. Yes, Lazarus. In his poverty
he was rich, in his wretchedness he was happy;
when he had nothing he possessed all things; and
when his misery seemed most complete, he was
nearest to endless life and joy.. What was it that
made him so blessed? It was true piety. Without that, his poverty had been the forerunner of
deeper poverty hereafter; and poor on earth, he
had been poorer still in hell. When he was destitute of food, and friends, and raiment, and shelter, he had one thing left, and that the one thing
needful. O my young friend, remember that if
you were as poor as Lazarus, as afflicted as Job
as persecuted as Paul, the love of Christ would

make you happy. And O, consider that without this you must be a miscrable wretch, though you were to live in wealth, pomp, and even royal splendor!

"Take another passage. Mark .ix. 46 : 'And if thy hand offend (*ensnare*) thee, cut it off : it is better for thee to enter into life maimed, than having two hands to go into hell, into the fire that never shall be quenched ; where their worm dieth not, and the fire is not quenched. And if thy foot offend (*ensnare*) thee, cut it off; it is better for thee to enter halt into life, than having two feet to be cast into hell, into the fire that never shall be quenched; where their worm dieth not, and the fire is not quenched. And if thine eye offend (*ensnare*) thee, pluck it out : it is better for thee to enter into the kingdom of God with one eye, than having two eyes to be cast into hell fire ; where their worm dieth not, and the fire is not quenched.' How solemn an admonition, to make every sacrifice for eternal life, is contained in this awful passage! Not only does the Son of God command you to part with toys and trinkets for his sake, but, to esteem no sacrifices nor sufferings too great when eternal life is at stake. It is as if he had said, " Salvation is the one thing needful ; and think nothing too precious to be resigned on its account : what though any thing as dear and important to you as the hand that earns your food, the foot on which you pursue your labors, the eye which warns you of a thousand dangers, and which is the source of a thousand satisfactions,—what though any thing thus dear and useful should ensnare your immortal soul, yet part with it ; yes, part with it, though it cost you as much exquisite torture to do so as it would to tear the tender eye from its socket, and to cut away the right hand and· foot from the body they support and adorn. Part with the dear cause of destruction, though through its loss the rest of your days were even to be spent in misery and want. Yet mind not the miseries of an hour to escape those of eternity; mind not all that a feeble body can endure, to escape the worm that never dieth, and the fire that never shall be quenched. Better, far better were it for you, to go, if needful, through pain, and want, and wretchedness, to heaven, than through comfort, and ease, and prosperity to hell."

Solemn and awakening charge! O that it were felt by every heart! Awful, awful warning, repeated six times by a compassionate Saviour, that there the fire never shall be quenched.

" Will you, my young friend, listen to his word? Will you, if you have not yet done so, now give your youth to God, and receive the blessed Jesus as your all in all? If you refuse, O may the God of mercy grant, that wherever you go in your mad career of business or of pleasure, the words of Christ may follow, and still thunder in your ear, that in that dismal abode, whither sin and folly lead the soul, the fire never shall be quenched! Flee, then, from it! Flee for your life! Flee for your soul! If milder motives have not moved you, what can awaken you, if this warning of the Lord's cannot? Flee from the dear delights of sin that are binding you over to perdition! They conduct you to that hell where the fire never, never shall be quenched! Flee from sins that have ruled you to the present hour, or they will shortly fix you where the worm of remorse and despair can never, never die!"

3

A PRAYER IMPLORING GRACE TO PAY DEVOUT ATTENTION
TO THIS SCRIPTURAL ADVICE.

O most holy, holy, holy Lord God, draw near
unto me, a sinner, in mercy, while I draw near unto
thee in a way of duty. I have done wickedly in
not hearkening to thy commandments. Alas, I have
disregarded the admonitions of thy word; I have
lived in sin all my days. I have profaned thy holy
day. I have profaned thy holy name. I have made
a mock at sin. I have never desired or attempted
to please thee, my God; I have pleased myself, and
have joined my sinful companions, and walked in
the way of the transgressor. It would be just in
thee, O Lord, to cut me off in the morning of my
days, and send me down to that world of woe,
"where their worm dieth not, and the fire is not
quenched." O, I shudder when I think how many
times I have made sport of those solemn warnings
in the Bible, in reference to eternal punishment.
I have believed what wicked men and wicked companions have said of the place of torment. O pardon this iniquity, for it is great. Cast me not off
forever from thy presence, but grant me the teach-
ings of the Holy Spirit, to convince me of sin, and
to renew, and sanctify, and save my soul, through
Jesus Christ, my Lord. *Amen.*

THE LOVE OF JESUS CHRIST.

"History relates, that one of those happy and
triumphant saints, who passed through the sorrows
of martyrdom to the glories of heaven, just before
he expired, lifting up his burning hands from the
midst of the flames, exclaimed, 'None but Christ,

none but Christ! But whence sprung this fervent love? the apostle's words reply, ' *we love him because he first loved us.* Spend then a few serious moments in meditating on the love of Jesus Christ, our Lord.

"Follow him, in your thoughts, from his throne of glory to his poor manger, and his bitter cross, and mark the painful steps he trod; then may you feel that never love was like his love, and never sorrow like his sorrow.

"He was the inhabitant of heaven before the world was formed. Eternal glory was his; all the riches of heaven were his portion; and angels and archangels bowed at his feet. He comes from a world where no sorrows enter, to a world of sorrow and distress. He wept over wretched men whom he saw ruining themselves for this world and the next. And O, my young friend, if you are unacquainted with his grace, were he upon earth again, he might weep for you. He would see your danger, if you saw it not. He would know the worth of your soul, though you knew it not, and would see, in all its horrors, the precipice whence you are falling, and the state of misery into which you are plunging. What an exchange has he made with wretched man! He bore our sorrows, that we might share his joys. He took our guilt, that we might partake of his righteousness; endured the bitterest agony, that we might escape eternal torments; died, that we might live; and came from heaven, that we might go and dwell forever there. O, then, remember, that when he was agonizing in the garden, crowned with thorns, torn with scourges, nailed to the cross, and writhing in misery there, that all this was on your account, and not his own.

"It is related of Colonel Gardiner, that at the time of his wonderful conversion, he thought that

there was before him a visible representation o'
our Lord Jesus Christ on the cross; and he was
impressed as if a voice had come to him to this effect; 'O sinner, did I suffer this for thee, and are
these thy returns?' If you, my young friend, have
hitherto neglected religion and the Son of God,
would he appear, might he not justly say the same,
to you? Is this your return for all this love?
And do you think the blessed Jesus endured the
less, or loved the less, because he is not here to
tell you the greatness of his sufferings and his
love? It cannot be; and will you then submit to
him? or will you still harden your heart in ingratitude and neglect? Consider this matter well, I
beseech you. Unless you turn to him, as far as
you are concerned, all this will be in vain. As to
you, it will be in vain that he came from heaven,
and became the poor man of sorrows. As to you,
it will be in vain that his hands, his feet, his side
were pierced, and that he became the sufferer of
the cross, the victim of death. O give him your
youth. Trust him with your soul. But if you
refuse to do this, if you continue to slight his love;
then, young sinner, expect hereafter no gentle
flames; no tolerable damnation: for know, that
the deepest and most wretched hell, will not be
more wretched than such iniquity will deserve."

A PRAYER OF A CONVICTED YOUTH.

"O thou compassionate Saviour, what praises,
what gratitude, I owe to thee! Why didst thou
stoop beneath the grave, to save a sinking world!
Why pass by sinful angels, to visit sinful men!
Why raise man to the heaven he never enjoyed.
and not restore them to the heaven they lost!

Why sink so low to raise us so high! Why suffer for such a worm as I! *Even so, Lord, for so it seemed good in thy sight.* Blessed Jesus, thy divine goodness undertook, thy power performed, this miracle of miracles. No merit didst thou see in man. None wilt thou ever see. Never can we repay the debt of gratitude. Never love thee half enough. O my injured God! my forgotten Saviour! my neglected soul! Had I ten thousand hearts, thy love demands them all; yet much of my life has passed, and angels and men have seen me denying thee this one poor unworthy heart. O gracious Saviour! O divine sacrifice! thou didst bleed for me; didst come to wash away my stains; to seek and save me who was lost. Let me live to thee; and in my life adorn thy Gospel and glorify thy name. Let me die to thee; and die with an assurance that I am thine; die, saying in my last hour, Beloved Saviour, through thy merits and thy death, a poor polluted worm, deserving hell, ascends to heaven. *Amen.*"

"Let me relate to you a little history, illustrative of the blessings of early piety.

"Some years since, in a village in Derbyshire, England, there lived a young and thoughtless girl: her name was Mary. Like most around her, she knew not God. Her days were chiefly spent in a cotton mill; and if a holiday came, it was an opportunity for vanity and sinful pleasure. Soon after she had completed her thirteenth year, the season for a wake at a neighboring village arrived; and she proposed to attend that season of dissipation and folly. A young woman, who had herself chosen the better part, persuaded Mary to accompany her to hear a sermon. She went. The place

3*

of.preaching was the cottage of a humble, aged
Christian, one of the Lord's poor. The preacher's
subject was, The *carnal mind is enmity againsi
God.* Mary˜listened ;the Lord opened her heart;
she felt the power of divine truth, in a way that
she never had done before; and left the house
with feelings very different from those which she
had on her entrance. She had done with the
wake. She felt herself deeply sinful and corrupt,
her mind was harrowed up with distress; and
eternal salvation became the object of her desires.
Now farewell to her former vanities and follies:
she forsook them forever; and from that evening
began to live anew. She sought, and at length
found peace in believing; and in her seventeenth
year was solemnly admitted into the church of
Christ. In this sacred connection she adorned
religion by consistent conduct; she prized her religious privileges; was affectionately attached to
her minister; and secured the esteem and regard
of her Christian friends. A few months after her
admission into the church of Christ, the symptoms
of a consumption appeared. and God quickly called
her to himself. In the days of languishing and
weakness, the Lord was her support She said
that she found his promises sweeter and sweeter;
that there are comforts and delights in his word,
which none know but those who enjoy them; and
that she never enjoyed so many blessings as during the time of her affliction. Death had lost his
threatening sting. 'I am not,' she said, 'afraid in
the least of dying any time.' At different times
she expressed her hope and peace; or called on
the friends that surrounded her dying bed, to
praise her God. At length she calmly entered into
rest, before she had spent eighteen years on earth.'

See, my young friend, how much the grace of God may do for them who embrace religion in early life, even in a little time. On her thirteenth birth-day, Mary was a thoughtless girl; and ere her eighteenth could arrive was a saint in light. With-in the intervening space of something more than four short years, she was enabled to forsake the world, to find a Saviour, to profess the Gospel, to honor that profession, to languish calmly through months of sickness, to conquer death, and doubt-less land in heaven. How blessed was early piety to her! She might, when first awakened, have said, 'I am not yet fourteen; surely hereafter will be soon enough for me;' and had she reasoned thus, and had she put off, though but for a few years, her inquiry for salvation, God, it seems, by her early death, would have put it off forever. De-lay not, then, to accept that blessing which is the source of every other. Your life is uncertain as was hers. If you, youthful reader, are a lover of this world, what will you have left soon? But if pos-sessed of religion, you may say, 'Not thus fleeting are my treasures.' ' *Thou art my portion, O Lord;* others have palaces, and crowns, or wealth, gayety, and pleasure. This is their portion; but thou, the God of heaven and earth, art mine, and mine for-ever. When the miser shall have lost his wealth, and crowns have fallen from the heads that wear them; when the man of this world shall have left the world he idolized, and all their delights shall have forsaken the young, the pleasure-taking, and the gay,—thou wilt still be mine: thou wilt be my support, when rocks crumble into dust, and mountains tremble to their base, and when the sun shall shine no more, and when the earth itself shall have vanished like a falling star, that blazes and expires—thou wilt be mine still, *my God ana my portion forever.*'

"And now were it possible to call from the dead some that have died in youth, O what a confirmation would they give, to all that has been urged upon you here! - They who have followed Jesus while young, might say to you, ' Follow him we followed. Early as we began religion, we began much too late, and could we have felt grief in heaven, we should have grieved that we did not sooner know, and love, and serve the Lord. Death cut us down in the morning of our days; yet we did not die too soon, for we had bowed betimes at the feet of Jesus, and had found eternal life in him. He washed our sins away, he renewed our hearts, and prepared heaven for us, and us for heaven. He taught us to set our affections on things above. We smiled in death : and now we rest from all our labors. Heaven is a long, long, happy home. Follow our Lord, and he will be your Lord. Receive him, and he will receive you. Commit your souls to him, and all will be well with you, for time and for eternity.' "

MEDITATIONS ON THE ADVANTAGES OF EARLY
PIETY CONCLUDED WITH PRAYER.

"Come, O my soul, and in serious meditation again review these pleasing motives for yielding thyself, thy all, to God. I am passing through this world like an eagle through the air. I am young; but youth and health have vanished from millions, and will soon vanish from me. Could I now gain a throne, and become a ruler of a mighty kingdom, yet in a little while a throne. a kingdom, will be of little importance to me : but I hear of things that will concern me forever, of blessings that may enrich me forever. I hear of treasures of eternal worth; treasures like those which angels enjoy, and which make angels happy. Thrones and kingdoms upon earth never will be mine, even for an hour ; but these far better riches may be mine through an eternal day. When Jesus invites me to go to him, and take his yoke, he invites me to make all this my own. And canst thou hesitate, O my soul, or canst thou delay? Shall I refuse so kind an invitation? Shall I lose all these eternal treasures, for the things of a moment, that perish in the using? O, let me not act so base, so foolish so unprofitable a part! I see, indeed, that godliness is profitable for all things, and would be infinitely profitable to me. Without it, I had better never had been born. Without it, I must be a mere cumberer of the ground. Then my very being would be a curse to myself; and I should be a curse to my friends, and a curse to the world ; but with it, in my humble sphere, I should be enabled to glorify my God ; I should live to my blessed Redeemer, and might die leaning, as it were, my languishing head for support upon his Almighty arm.

"Great, and ever blessed God, from revolving these things in my mind, to thee would I turn. O, let them not be lost upon me ; let these precious blessings all be mine. Deny me other treasures, if thou wilt, but give me these. Let me win Christ,' and know him as mine, and know all the blessings which flow from his love, either on earth, or in heaven, as also mine. Give me the comfort of hope, the assurance of faith, and the heaven of love, which is the forerunner of the earnest of an eternal heaven, within me, and around

me, when time shall be no more. Let me not, by
delay, make repentance more bitter, and conversion
more difficult; but may I feel true humility and
sorrow for having wasted, and worse than wasted, so
much of my life ; and again let me entreat thee to
give me grace, gladly to yield the rest to thee. Or
if, O compassionate Father, thou seest that I have
been led to this happy choice, then confirm me in
it, and never let sin or the world-divide the bands
which bind my soul to thee'; but may I be blessed
in Jesus, and humbly and faithfully cleave to him.
Grant me but these blessings, and then make whatever pleases thee welcome to me. Let afflictions
be welcome, as the chastisement of thy hand, and
pain, as sent to meeten me for the rest where there
shall be no more pain.' If thou art pleased to pro-
long my days, let life be welcome, for the sake of
living to my Lord. But if thou hast determined
otherwise respecting me, if a few weeks or months
are to finish my pilgrimage below, let even early
death be welcome, as a speedier removal to eternal
life ; and let those years which are taken from my
mortal course, be added to that eternal day, to
which thou hast promised to conduct all the humble followers of thy Son. Great God, thou seest
nothing in me to add weight to these requests ;
and never wilt thou see such worthiness in a creature so unworthy ; but grant them for his sake
whose blood was shed to wash away my sins.
Amen."

THE HAPPY CONCLUSION OF A RELIGIOUS
LIFE, A MOTIVE FOR EARLY PIETY.

"O, my young friend, let me tell you seriously
that you must die, and unless you obtain the con

solations of religion, must know their importance when too late. O, happy, happy they who die in the Lord. Let the vain world keep its possessions! Let the fashionable and the gay enjoy their short-lived gayety, and quickly ending pleasure! Let the wealthy exult in their stores, and the noble in their honors! these are not the happy. The solemn death-bed, where the humble, faithful disciple of Jesus has lain, has often afforded a happier spectacle than the most happy ever beheld in scenes of worldly revelry and pleasure.

"Perhaps you look on death as dreadful; but many as young as you have met it without a fear; and without a wish to stay long here, have passed through that important hour to life, to happiness, to Jesus, heaven, and God. In 1808, died H. S. Colding, in the 24th year of his age. When he felt the approach of death, he is stated to have uttered these rapturous expressions: 'I find now it is no delusion! My hopes are well founded! Eye hath not seen, nor ear heard, neither hath it entered into the heart of man to conceive the glory I shall shortly partake of! Read your Bible! I shall read mine no more—no more need it!' When his brother said to him, 'You seem to enjoy foretastes of heaven:'—'O,' replied he, 'this is no longer foretaste—this is heaven! I not only feel the climate, but breathe the air of heaven, and shall soon enjoy the company! Can this be dying? This body seems no longer to belong to the soul! it appears only as a curtain that covers it; and soon I shall drop the curtain, and be set at liberty!' Then, putting his hand to his breast, he exclaimed, 'I rejoice to feel these bones give way, as it tells me I shall be with my God in glory.'

"The last words that he was heard to utter were 'Glory, glory, glory.'"

In July, 1827, died, at an early age, a young disciple of the Saviour, related to the eminent missionary, Mr. Ward. Her name was Jane. When about fifteen, she embraced religion, and sought peace in a Saviour's love, encouraged by the gracious promise, "Come unto me all ye that labor and are heavy laden, and I will give you rest."

"Some expressions written by that mouldering hand may teach the young the worth of early piety. *I am in perfect health*, but not knowing how soon death may come. I am hastening to the grave, but not with sorrow; for I know in whom I have believed, that he is able to keep what I have committed unto him. I must soon part with all below and with my dear minister, but not forever; for I hope we shall soon meet in Christ, and part no more.'

"Her last illness was long and painful. Many hours of severe distress did she pass in her sick chamber, on her bed of death, but all was peace within. Often did she express her confidence in her Saviour, which at times rose to the full assurance of faith. 'My mind is very happy—in a very happy frame, and a thankful frame. I have no exultation, but I know that if all the world were lost, I should be saved.' She anticipated, with comfort, an entrance in her heavenly Father's home. With all this gladdening confidence was manifested deep humility: 'I am,' she said, 'an unworthy sinner, and have done nothing for my salvation.' In her last hours, when the power of speech was almost gone, she faintly whispered, 'Happy,' and seemed in prayer to say, 'Come, my dear Saviour.' Shall you die thus? Can you die thus, unless you seek the Saviour as yours, and yield, like Jane, your youth to him?

"Youthful reader, you too must die; yet if possessed of a humble assurance that Jesus is your Saviour, you may die in peace. O! when this scene of vanity is ending; when all your ornaments must be exchanged for a shroud, and all the amusements of youth, or the cares of riper years, for the solemnities of the eternal world, then, indeed, will early piety appear a blessing past expression. If you are a Christian, you too may be able to say at the closing scene of life, 'Farewell folly, sin, and vanity!' Farewell all that I once knew!—I go where perfection and purity, happiness and endless life, shall be my long, long portion. I go from mortal to immortal things; from dying men to the living God. Adieu! forever, departing world, adieu! But O, welcome, ye blessed spirits, that come to convey me to my God! Welcome ye blissful scenes of peace, and love, and joy, and praise! Welcome heaven! Welcome everlasting life!

PROV. VIII. 17.

1. " Ye hearts, with youthful vigor warm,
　　In smiling crowds draw near,
　　And turn from every mortal charm,
　　A Saviour's voice to hear.

2. " He, Lord of all the worlds on high,
　　Stoops to converse with you;
　　And lays his radiant glories by,
　　Your friendship to pursue.

3 " The soul that longs to see my face,
　　Is sure my love to gain;
　　And those that early seek my grace,
　　Shall never seek in vain.

4

4. " What obj ect, Lord, my soul should move
    If one; compared with thee ?
    What beauty should command my love,
    Like what in Christ I see ?

5. ' Away ye false, delusive toys,
    Vain tempters of the mind!
    Tis here I fix my lasting choice,
    And here true bliss I find.

A SEA INFIDEL CONVERTED.

" THE following interesting letter was addressed
to the Rev. G. C. Smith, of London, by a sailor
who had been an inmate of the New Sailor's Asylum, opened under Mr. Smith's auspices."

" REVEREND SIR,—I humbly beg that you will
pardon the liberty I take in thus addressing you;
I am convinced that you *will*, when you learn the
subject and circumstances which induce me to ad
dress you. The subject is one in which you are
deeply interested—the regeneration of the human
soul ; and the circumstances are, the conversion of
a man who has been a long time estranged from
his God ; 'a dweller in the tents of sin ;' familiar
with, and addicted to vice and depravity ; and most
grievous of all, who had abjured and denied his
God and Saviour ; who has poured forth from his
mouth, as from the crater of hell, torrents of blas-
phemy ; and embraced and eagerly sought every
opportunity of turning the Holy Scriptures, and
the religion of Christ, into ridicule and contempt.

" Such has been the man, sir, who now addresses
you ; such were the practices I persevered and glo-

ried in for upwards of twenty years. Now it has pleased the omniscient and all-merciful God, to awaken me to a sense of my guilt; to cast from my eyes the film of delusion; and to turn away the clouds of darkness which have caused me to grope blindly along through the valley of destruction and death; a measure of divine grace has been imparted; a change I have experienced; a happy, I trust in God, an effectual change. Ah me! when I look back on my past wicked life, the review is dreadful; my soul recedes and shudders at the awful remembrance. I have been standing on the brink of a precipice, ready in a moment to fall headlong below, into the dark and unfathomable abyss, where my destruction must have been inevitable and eternal.

"On my first obtaining, through the favor and grace of God, a view and a sense of my lost condition; my sins, my blasphemies, and my impieties, sprang up like torturing fiends around me. My soul was agonized and frantic; I considered myself as deservedly and eternally lost. I gave myself up to dark despair. I wished,—pardon me, sir, the expression of the dreaded idea,—I wished myself annihilated; I wished I could regain the opinions I had so lately held; but ever thankful shall I be to divine mercy, I could not; I assayed again and again, but they had fled from a more heavenly presence. The good and evil spirits were at war within me; the light of divine truth prevailed; and the Satanic ties were burst which so long had bound me.

"I repaired to the Scriptures for spiritual comfort;—the Holy Scriptures, that volume of truth which I had so long despised, that volume which I had lately thrown from me with detestation, I

now pressed close to my bosom ; I opened its pages
and read that Christ died as an atonement for sinners, for the chief of sinners. ' Though their sins
are as red as scarlet, they shall be made white as
wool ;' he invites all to come to him,—' to knock.
and it shall be opened ;' 'to seek, and they shall
find ;' to ' believe in him and they shall be saved.'

" I am now calm ; I believe that I can yet hope
for pardon through the intercession of our blessed
Saviour. ' There is joy over one sinner that re-
penteth, more than over ninety and nine just persons that have not sinned, and need not repentance.' I will seek the divine presence with .hope,
yet with 'fear and trembling.' I will not sink in
the gloom and darkness of despair, nor will I be
vainly elated with too presumptive hopes of salva
tion. Sincere contrition for past sins and iniquities; a firm belief in the sacred truths of divine
revelation ; prayer and supplication, humbly offered up through the mediation of Jesus Christ
the Redeemer ; these, I conceive. sir, are the sacrifices I should offer up to the offended Majesty
of heaven ; these can alone be my plea, when ar-
raigned at the bar of that awful tribunal, before
that all-powerful Judge, ' to whom the heart of
man is known, and his most secret thoughts.'

" To you, sir, and your brother ministers, I owe
a debt of eternal gratitude. You have been the
means through which God has been pleased to work
my deliverance from the state of spiritual death,
from the horrid, all-damning principles I had so
long embraced; it was to your preaching, and the
Spirit of grace working internally my conviction,
that I owe the present happiness of my soul.
Lately, I had esteemed myself as one of the bru-
tal creation, as a beast of the field ; beyond this

earth I had no hopes or fears; beyond the laws and usages of society, I knew of no inducement to seek virtue, or to deter from crime; no inward monitor; no appeal of conscience. Could I conform to the laws of mankind, I thought I was guiltless and unpuuishable for any action, however base. This, in my opinion, sir, merely as a point of human reasoning, shows the necessity of divine revelation; I am convinced that a community of infidels could not exist as a state of society.

" When we lose sight of divine revelation and a superintending Providence, we have no guide but nature and the impulse of our blind passions : we are lost; we may be compared to the mariner in a ship, on an unknown sea ; tempest-driven, no chart, no compass to direct his course, and conduct his helm.

" I will endeavor, sir, as briefly as possible, to give you a sketch of my life during the last twenty years. The record of sin is a gloomy subject; but is yet interesting; much so to me, as a beacon to warn me in my future course, or as a torturing, but inseparable friend, to goad and drive me forward to the goal of expiation.

" My parents were sober and pious people; they brought me up in a strict attention to religious principles, and frequent reading of the Holy Scriptures. Ah! had I never forsook the path they inculcated, I had been happy; but Satan is permitted to prowl the earth, seeking whom he may devour, and I became his victim.

" About the age of fifteen, some of the writings of Hume and Voltaire fell into my hands ; a fatal bias by these was given to my mind. From these I inhaled the pestilential blasts of infidelity. I sought with avidity for sceptical writings; I ran

4*

through a host of these baneful authors, and *they* completed my ruin.

"The steps of evil are progressive. I did not for some time avow my change of principles; I was ashamed, I was even affrighted of them. I was most careful, in particular, to conceal them from my parents. O, sir, it is still a consolation to my mind that I did so; it would have sent their gray hairs with sorrow to the grave. They knew it not while in this mortal vale; they would have been frantic could they have imagined that their son had denied his God.

"The principles I had adopted at this time, sir, were *deism*, as such, I believe, it is commonly understood; a belief in a God, or first cause, but disbelief in divine revelation, and the immortality of the soul. But I stopped not long here; I embraced *materialism*. The transition is easy, and I became an *atheist*.

"Whatever difference the names of *deist* and *atheist* may seem to imply, they are radically the same; *atheism* is the goal to which all infidelity tends. When we reject revelation and divine providence, where is our God? When we deny spiritual existence, who is he?

"I embraced a sea-faring life, and have followed it for upwards of twenty years. Ah! during this time the evil I have been the author of, in poisoning the minds of my shipmates, is incalculable. I have been, sir, a firebrand, an incendiary, a demon. I have argued with those that would argue with me, against the truth of Christianity, and where argument failed me in carrying my point, I resorted to satire and ridicule. Alas! I fear I have too far succeeded; that on the awful day we must all see, some unhappy souls will denounce me as the author of their eternal ruin; but God in Christ is merciful, and knows the weakness of the human heart of man. To him I look for pardon.

"Yet during this period of mental blindness and infatuation, which had swept me away, a spark of divine truth, which had been early planted in my bosom, lay there suppressed and smothered, but could not be extinguished. It often called me to account for the sinful course I was pursuing, but I hastened and always succeeded in crushing its expanding influence. I would thus say to myself, 'Psha! those phantasies are only the prejudices of education, working on a feeble mind. I will conjure them away;—I will philosophize them from me. It is like the man who in his youth has listened to tales of ghosts and spectres; his better sense tells him of the non-existence of such phantoms, but in certain situations he cannot divest himself of fear.' By such sophisms as these, sir, I endeavored to stifle the groans of a suffering conscience within me.

"Once on a similar occasion, I recollect having thus addressed myself: 'Why should I be tormented thus by unaccountable fears, doubts, and waverings? Elijah is represented as having said to his countrymen, "Men of Israel, how long halt ye between two opinions? If the Lord be God, follow him." I will similarly say to himself. Victim of incertitude! how long will I dwell between two opinions? If the Scriptures are truth, follow them; and if there is no law but that of nature, follow it.'

"In spite of every inward remonstrance and solemn warning, in spite of dangers and disasters by shipwreck and by fire, in spite of the howl of

the midnight tempest, and the roar of battle, an
infatuated victim of sceptical delusion, I remained
a confirmed and hardened sinner.   Satan was yet
permitted to hold dominion over my callous heart.

" I never attended divine worship, and by example or by derision endeavored to deter others.   I
compared it in my mind to a serpent which I well
knew possessed a sting which might wound me.
If worship was held on board, I always contrived
to avoid it ; if on shore, I never visited a church
but to scoff, and to catch some topic or expression
of the preacher, which I might turn to ridicule.

" I was once of the crew of the Lady Carrington,
in a voyage to the East Indies.   I and some of my
associates engaged in the formation of a weekly
paper, which was styled ' The Carrington Nautic
Chronicle.'   It was generally produced on a Sunday, and affixed on some conspicous part of the
gun-deck, for the inspection of the crew.   Such a
plan as this, sir, if properly conducted on moral
and religious principles, might prove of great benefit in the instruction of seamen, in long voyages ;
but in this instance, when you consider, sir, that
my associates were men of my own *caste*, you will
perceive that ours must have been of pernicious influence.   Truly it was so ; demoralizing and irreligious, and our subjects were obscene, profane,
and blasphemous.   I have in several vessels since
pursued the same unhallowed course.

" I will now, sir, draw my narrative to a close.
I have latterly, for some years, sailed mostly in
foreign vessels.   Returning to this country, like
many of my improvident brothers, my dissolute
courses soon brought me to a state of distress.
Forced to seek shelter, I sought and obtained it
in the Asylum, and what I considered as the great-

est calamity that had befallen me, has proved, under the blessing of God, the happiest circumstance
of my life. It is here that I have been brought to
a just sense of my long-lost condition; it is here,
sir, that my ears have been first arrested to listen
to the joyful tidings of salvation; that my eyes
have been first riveted to the 'sacred page, and
that my heart has first opened to receive the impression of a solemn warning to 'flee from the
wrath to come.' I humbly beg, sir, if I am not
too presumptive, that you will write to me on the
subject of this letter, such advice and instruction
as you may deem necessary. If I have advanced
any thing, sir, wrong in principle or in diction, I
hope you will ascribe it to its true source—to ignorance or mistake; surely it cannot be otherwise.
With sincere feelings of gratitude and respect, I
am, your most obèdient and humble servant.

"G."

"P. S. It may be necessary to state that, you
now have my true name. In consequence of the
dissolute and unprincipled course of life I had
hitherto led, I have seldom passed by my proper
name; that under which I entered the Asylum is
a false one. To explain what you have already
received, you should know that when I belonged
to the Inconstant frigate, on the coast of Africa, I
conducted a paper there on the plan of that mentioned above in the Carrington."

Sailor's Mag.

THE CROSS IS MY ANCHOR.

THE CROSS IS MY ANCHOR,—though wave follow wave,
Though frail be my vessel, this anchor shall save.
Let faith in full confidence trust in the Lord;
Midst dangers I rest on his life-giving word.

" THE CROSS IS MY ANCHOR,—'tis steady and sure,
Within the vail holding all storms I endure ;
My Jesus has entered a priest on His throne,
I trust in His promise, and in Him alone.

" THE CROSS IS MY ANCHOR,—All storms shall soon cease,
And my vessel, though frail, reach the haven of peace ;
No shipwreck or storm need I ever more fear,
When danger's extreme, then my Saviour is near.

" THE CROSS IS MY ANCHOR,—i now hear His voice,
' It is I,' then I fear not, but trust and rejoice ;
·'he last storm with its low'ring, may speedily come,
I'll trust in His cross, and shall soon reach my home.

" THE CROSS IS MY ANCHOR "

Lines Addressed to the Author of the Above.

" IF THE CROSS BE THY ANCHOR,—thy pilot must be
The Saviour that walked on the fathomless sea ;
That reproved and controlled the proud waves at His will
And spoke ' Peace' to the tempest, and bade it ' be still.'

" IF THE CROSS BE THY ANCHOR,—no harm can be hurled
On thy head when the whirlwind is vexing the world ;
Innoxious the flash shall disfigure the sky,
And the red bolt of ruin pass harmlessly by.

" IF THE CROSS BE THY ANCHOR,—by sceptic abhorred,
And thy cable the ne'er-failing word of the Lord,
Thy voyage is safe and thy haven secure,
And for time and eternity thou shalt endure.

" IF THE CROSS BE THY ANCHOR,—then blest be thy lot,
For the crash of creation shall injure thee not ;
With the trump that shall wake the wide world with alarms
Thy Saviour will hasten thee home to his arms.

Sailor's Magazine.   O. M.

THE SEAMEN'S CAUSE.

Extract from a speech at one of the English Anniversaries.

" HE looked back to the time when efforts wore first made in behalf of seamen, and he thought the fathers and mothers of sailors were like the prophet upon Mount Carmel; they had fallen upon their faces and had wrestled with God in prayer. Many a father, like the Rev. A. Fuller, whose son Robert was perishing amidst sin and wretchedness, found a very heaven; and many a parent, like the Rev. Leigh Richmond, whose beloved son had gone to sea, and had caused many an aching heart to his pious family, had implored the blessing of God upon sailors; and the Christians of the present day had seen the result of it, when the cloud arose out of the midst of the sea. He thought such characters would say, ' Go, look toward the sea.' If they were asked why they directed their attention to the sea, they would reply. because they had a prodigal son, over whom their bowels yearned. Christians of the present day had seen the cloud arise; they hailed it in London, and, like the message of the prophet sent to Ahab, they said, ' Haste, thou, and go down, for there is a sound of abundance of rain.' The cloud was like a man's hand, but the faith of the prophet realized it, and he knew that it was the precursor of greater blessings. His servant ran before the chariot, and cried, ' Rain, rain, rain.' Twelve years ago the cloud was seen rising, and there was the sound of abundance of rain; but if Christians supposed they had only to embark the vessel, and that they should always have a fair wind and a full tide in the sailor's cause, they would be mistaken. Many rocks and shoals had been met with, but they were perfectly natural. They had, however, only given a new turn to the thoughts and a fresh direction to the exertions of the friends of seamen. They had run on board a rock, and were backing the vessel off, but it was not their intention always to run astern; on the contrary, they meant to leave the rocks to the larboard, and then go on again. (Cheers.) The cause was still the same, and it could not be altered. It was the cause of truth, righteousness and peace; the cause of God against the empire of Satan; and it was their duty to promote it, notwithstanding all their enemies. Satan had seen the Gospel carried to the villages of his country; he had witnessed its dissemination in heathen lands; but when he saw it promulgated among seamen, he felt that it was a death-blow to his empire."

THE PIOUS CAPTAIN'S PRAYER AND REFLECTIONS WHILE AT SEA.

O Lord, I acknowledge that I am less than the least of thy mercies. I have forfeited every right to thy compassion; I have strayed from thee like a lost sheep; I confess that my sins have provoked thee to withdraw from me thy wonted favor. Thou, O God, hast justly hedged up my way, and made my paths crooked. Yet I thank thee, O thou God of mercy, that a ray of hope is still afforded me under the darkness of my mind. and the hidings of thy face. I thank thee that I am permitted to indulge the consoling reflection that there is for-

giveness with thee, that thou mayest be feared. I
pray, O Lord, that the necessities of my case may
plead for my importunity, and that thou wouldst
verify thy promises of faithfulness and truth, where-
in thou hast caused me to hope, and carry on thy
begun goodness to me, O Lord, until I can say,
with thy servant of old, "Lord, thou knowest all
things, thou knowest that I love thee." Will the
Lord hear my prayer, and attend unto my cry, for
his own holy name's sake; and to the only wise God,
Father, Son, and Spirit, I would render everlasting
praises. *Amen.*

"I am sensible that my case, as it respects my
spiritual condition, calls for extraordinary thought-
fulness and solemnity; and as a remedy has been
provided for such helpless sinners, I apply to that
remedy with all that solicitude and diligence which
my peculiar situation requires. In looking over
my journal, I find that, about eleven years since,
I was much oppressed with doubts and fears, and
that after laboring under these difficulties of mind
for some time, I resolved to seek unto God, by fasting and prayer, for relief. The Lord was gracious
to me, and delivered me from all my fears and apprehensions. Am I not, then, encouraged to look
to him, in the same way, for the removal of my
present distresses, and that he would once more
set my soul at liberty from the bondage of sin and
death, and cause me to rejoice in his salvation?
But it is not my past experience only that I feel
encouraged to hope and wait on the Lord, by renewed importunity, for a favorable change; but by
the solemn exhortations and promises of the Lord
himself. For he says, in the second chapter of
Joel, 'Therefore also now, saith the Lord, turn
ye even to me with all your heart, and with fasting,

5

and with weeping, and with mourning; and rend
your heart, and not your garments, and turn unto
the Lord your God ; for he is gracious and merciful, slow to anger, and of great kindness, and re-
penteth him of the evil.' Who knoweth if he will
return and repent, and leave a blessing behind
him. And again, in the sixth chapter of Matthew,
our Saviour teaches, not only how to fast accepta-
bly, but promises important blessings in answer to
the performance of this duty. Hoping in the mercy
and faithfulness of God, I am resolved, by the assistance of his grace, to seek unto him more earnestly and fervently, until he be pleased to appoint
unto me beauty for ashes, the oil of joy for mourning, and the garment of praise for the spirit of
heaviness ; and O, may I experience all this mercy for his name's sake."—*Sailor's Magazine.*

THE COMPASS.

" The storm was loud—before the blast
    Our gallant bark was driven ;
Their foaming crests the billows reared,
And not one friendly star appeared
    Through all the vault of heaven.

" Yet dauntless still the steersman stood,
    And gazed without a sigh,
Where, poised on needle bright and slim,
And lighted by a lantern dim,
    The compass meets his eye.

" Thence taught his darksome course to steer,
    He breathed no wish for day ;
But braved the whirlwind's headlong might,
Nor once throughout that dismal night,
    To fear or doubt gave way.

And what is oft the Christian's life,
    But storms as dark and drear,

Through which, without one blithesome ray
Of worldly bliss to cheer his way,
He must his vessel steer!

" Yet let him ne'er to sorrow yield,
For in the sacred page
A compass shines divinely true,
And self-illumined, greets his view
Amid the tempest's rage.

" Then firmly let him grasp the helm,
Though loud the billows roar,
And soon his toils and troubles past,
His anchor he shall safely cast
On Canaan's happy shore."

Sailor's Magazine.

WORSHIP AT SEA.

The following Discourse was given by the shipmaster to his ship's company while on the voyage.

"So the shipmaster came to him, and said unto him, What meanest thou, O sleeper? Arise, call upon thy God, if so be that God will think upon us, that we perish not.—JONAH i. 6.

" Once more we are permitted to assemble together to worship God, and I hope we may lose nothing by devoting a small part of this day to the public worship of Jehovah. I am sure we should be gainers if we gave a part of every day to his service. But in order that we may fix our minds on this subject more steadily, I have chosen a text of that Scripture which was given by the inspiration of God, and is profitable to us according to the use we make of it. The prophet Jonah, as we read, was sent to preach to the great city of Nineveh: but fearing man more than God, he was determined not to go. He went down to

Joppa and found a vessel going to Tarshish, and paid his passage and went to sea in her. Now the Lord sometimes permits men to go certain lengths in sin, to try them. But they must come to judgment some time or other, either in this world, or the world to come ; and happy are they who like Jonah, return before it is for ever too late, and judge themselves, and acknowledge they have sinned.

" In the text before us we have an instance of faith, even in heathen men, which ought to put many, even professing Christians, to the blush. Hear the shipmaster exclaiming, 'What meanest thou, O sleeper ? Arise, call upon thy God !' Let us take a lesson from this heathen, my friends.

" And in the first place, let us consider whether we do not need the assistance of God as much as these men. They were idolaters, it is true, and went each man to his own god, and cried to him. But they found that their dumb god's did not still the tempest. They were sailors, and perhaps as like us in their dispositions, in their manners, in their evil habits, and in all things except their dress. as we can well imagine. They were sensible that there was an overruling power, and believed that if they wanted to be saved, they must ask. In this, they rather differed from many in these times. There are, strange as it may appear, in these times, men who say that if they are to be saved, they shall be saved, whether they accept or refuse the invitation that God daily makes to them. But these seamen, of which our text speaks, certainly went before us in candor ; and after finding it availed them nothing to cry to their gods, they went to Jonah ; who, we read, was asleep in the side of the ship, as unconcerned as if he had been doing to the utmost the will of God.

"They did not say, we had rather perish than be saved by the God of Jonah; as I fear too many in these days do,—at least in their actions. But they even admonished him for his irreligion, and begged of him to arise and call upon his God. It was a custom with these people at that time, when a person was suspected of any crime, and it could not be determined who that person was, to draw lots. As the Scripture says, 'The lot is cast into the lap, but the whole disposal thereof is of the Lord.' Accordingly they drew lots, and it fell to Jonah. They immediately inquired who, and what he was, and why they were visited with this dispensation of Providence. Jonah very ingenuously confesses the whole. Then they inquire what they shall do to him in order to appease the anger of God. He tells them to throw him overboard. How dreadfully he must have felt, when death was desirable, rather than the wrath of an angry God! But mark the result. The heathen, who had never known the one only and true God before, now see, and acknowledge his power to rule the winds and the waves. They accordingly, when they get ashore again, offer sacrifices, and make vows to God.

Jonah we should suppose would never be heard from again. But Jonah saw that he had done wrong, and confessed his sins to God, and prayed to be delivered, and God heard him, and delivered him even from the jaws of death. Now, as seamen, do we not need the assistance of God as much as these men? Can we say we are not idolaters as well as they? Perhaps we do not bow

5*

down to *graven images.* But do we not love any
thing better than God?

"Who among us denies himself of one worldly
lust for the sake of God? Who does not worship
one or the other of the gods of this world? Then
take a lesson from these heathen mariners, that in
the day of God's wrath, these gods cannot save
you. You may cry unto the god of lust, the god
of avarice, or the god of ambition· and which of
them can save you in the hour of death? We
know that there is but one only living and true
God. And we know that this God is a *holy* God,
and that we must be holy in order to please him.
And when we come to leave this world none of us
will regret having lived too near to God.

"It is appointed unto man once to die, and after death the judgment. Are we to escape death?
Although we have passed through so many dangers, yet we need not presume from that, that
death will never come. Perhaps, after escaping
many a storm at sea, and many a shipwreck, and
having weathered out many a sickly climate, yet
in such an hour as we think not, the Son of Man
cometh. We may be in a snug harbor at home,
and feel ourselves safe, yet the time is coming
when we little think; and then, where shall we
go? Is not the same God who rules the winds
and the waves, able to save or destroy? Has he
not the same power now that he had in Jonah's
day? Alas! it is in vain for me to try to persuade you to save your souls against your own
wills; therefore I leave you in the hands of God,
praying him to have mercy on you, for Christ's
sake.

"But allow me to tell you, that if you and I are
not saved, it is not because we have not had warn-

ing enough. It is not because the Lord would not help us; it is not because Christians do not desire our salvation; it is not because Christ has not done all that was possible, as a Saviour, he could do; it is not because the Spirit of God has no compassion upon us. No: it is simply because we do not wish to be saved.

"But I seem to hear you say, 'We *do* wish to be saved.' Well, then, show by your actions that you wish to be saved. If you were on a wreck at sea, and had not the means of subsistence, were in a state of starvation, and no hope of escaping the jaws of death, if in this situation, while you had just given up the last ray of hope, and was about to lay yourself down and die, you should discover in the horizon *a sail*, making towards you, and if upon her coming up, she should send a boat to rescue you from your forlorn condition, do you think that you would refuse to go on board of the stanch ship, and leave your deplorable wreck, and insist on their taking the wreck in tow, and leave you on board of her? Would not such conduct be unreasonable? So, and much more so, is the conduct of men, who find themselves adrift upon the ocean of time, in a body completely wrecked with sin, and their souls are starving for the righteousness of Christ. Behold! in the spiritual horizon a stately vessel heaves in sight! It is the ark of safety. Will you refuse to leave your self-righteous wreck? Do you expect the Captain of salvation to take your old wreck of sin in tow, and tow you into heaven in that state? You cannot be so unreasonable.

"You understand the Scripture, where our Saviour says, 'Ye must be born again.' 'Therefore, if any man be in Christ he is a new creature'

Now this boat is alongside, waiting your reply.
Will you enter the ark of safety, or dare you stay
another night adrift upon the ocean of life, and
your body so wrecked with sin as soon to sink your
soul with it, to everlasting woe ?   Perhaps if you
wait until to-morrow, you may have neither opportunity nor inclination to attend to your souls."

LORD, HEAR THE SEAMAN'S CRY.

' Awaked from gentlest midnight sleep,
  I hear the howling blast;
The chamber rocks—the murmur deep
  Of ocean, rises fast.
The lurid flash, the thunder's roar,
  Proclaim the tempest nigh,
And wavering lights are off our shore—
  ' Lord, hear the seaman's cry !'

This hour, perhaps, the sailor thinks,
  Of wife or mother far,
As drenched and spiritless, he shrinks,
  At some portentous bar.
The cresting foam betokens death;
  The breaker's rage is nigh :
He prays, with quick, redoubled breath;
  ' Lord, hear the seaman's cry !'

' Ah ! many a youth now lost in sin,
  And many a hoary sire,
Who never prayed, this night begin
  To dread Almighty ire.
In headlong fury while the bark
  Pierces the billows high,
They learn to pray in anguish—hark !
  ' Lord, hear the seaman's cry !'

" Though sinking in the whelming flood,
  In solitary woe,
Saviour ! thy ever-precious blood
  Can reach thy hapless foe—

Catch the faint, smothered voice of him
   Whose penitential sigh
Rises amid the terror grim :—
   ' Lord, hear the seaman's cry !'

" Pray for the sailor, ye who rest
   Upon your curtained bed :
Pray to the Power at whose behest
   The fearful storm hath sped.
And when, released from fear and care,
   Sweet hours of night glide by,
Be sometimes this your fervent prayer
   ' Lord, hear the seaman's cry !' "

Sailor's Magazine.

THE WAY TO BE SAVED.

Neither is there salvation in any other, for there is none other name
under heaven given among men whereby we must be saved."
ACTS iv. 12.

" IN the context we are told, ' as they spake unto
the people, the priests, and the captain of the temple, and the Sadducees, came upon them, (that is,
the apostles,) being grieved that they taught the
people, and preached, through Jesus, the resurrection from the dead.'

" The rulers, and priests, and great men among
the Jews, had not so much objection to the Bible,
to the apostles' preaching, to the disciples' doing
good, if it was done in some other name than the
name of Christ. But in the text we are told that
there is none other, &c. It is only by Christ, and
his name, that those favors can be expected from
God which are necessary to our salvation. This is
the honor of Christ's name, that it is the only name
whereby we must be saved. The only name we
have to plead in all our addresses to God. This

name is given ; God has appointed it. It is given *under heaven.* Christ has not only a great name *in heaven,* but a great name *under heaven;* for he has all power, both in the upper and lower world. It is given *among men* who need salvation ; men who are ready to perish. We may be saved by this name, and we cannot be saved by any other. From this subject, I observe,

"FIRST, *We must be saved.*

" I want the young : I want every person who is in the full vigor of life : I want every aged person : I want myself: I want us all to feel, (said the preacher) that we *must* be *saved.* For if I am not saved, I shall be *lost.* If I am not a partaker of Divine grace, I shall shortly be a partaker of Divine wrath. If I am not shortly saved, I shall soon be eternally lost! If affliction should come and overtake me in my sins, and if death should follow, as the messenger of God, I should be lost, forever and ever! Do, hearer, think of this!

" I want every one personally to think thus. Don't say this subject concerns some of my neighbors. Don't evade the force of truth by such vain opinions. But do think, I beseech you, that if you are not personally saved, in a very short time, you will be personally lost, and lost forever! I do not want you, when you are thinking of this subject, to say to yourselves, I hope that many heard what the minister said to-day, for I could tell many things which they have done, which they ought not to have done. Do not think of them ; no, do not think of them, I say, but to pray for them. Think, Oh! think of this : *I must* be *saved.* For, if I am not saved. I must be *lost.*

" It often affects my heart when I pass through the streets and among boats and vessels, and see the crowds of people that are passing along. In fifty years, scarcely one out of one hundred of them will be in this world. In forty years, almost all of this multitude will have been conveyed into another world—eternally lost. or eternally saved! Let such a consideration as this impress your minds when you see the crowds that are passing along, and offer up a short prayer that they may be saved. Do more than this; think, with reference to yourselves, that, 'Now is the accepted time; now is the day of salvation,' and that if you do not attend to the things that belong to your peace, you will not be saved, but will be *lost*, and lost forever!

" Do not think that there is no possibility that *you* may be lost, for it is absolute fact. It is not a case to be argued, whether you are in a lost state, or whether you are in a state of salvation; because, by the fall, and by actual transgression, we are all in a state of condemnation. It is true that we are not now, at this moment, in a world where hope never comes; but it is also true, that we may very soon be in that world, if we are not saved. I do not say this, (said the preacher,) because I know any thing of your personal characters, but because I know personal wickedness. I know the depravity of the heart; and that if we must be saved, it must be through Christ. For there is none other name under heaven given among men; and if we are not saved through Christ, then we are lost! irrecoverably lost!

" Fellow-candidates for eternity! pray for mercy in Christ. Pray that you may be saved, with as much individual particularity as if there was no other person on earth besides yourself. Say to yourselves, Am I saved? am I an heir of heaven? am I a child of God? am I a penitent, renewed

sinner? Do not say, If I should die this night
I should go to heaven, without considering the necessary qualifications for that world; but rather
inquire, Am I really in a saved state? Say, as I
hope I can say, that I dare not go to rest, I dare
not shut my eyes this night, unless I am comforta-
bly persuaded that I really am a poor saved sinner, through the Lord Jesus Christ. This, then,
is the first part of our subject,—*we must be saved.*

"*Secondly.* Salvation is possible. Guilty as we
are, condemned as we are, sinful as we are, wicked
as we are, and wretched as we are, this is the
name through which we may be saved. Though
we never can save ourselves, yet there is a Saviour
that can do it. It is not only certain that we must
be saved in this way, if we are saved at all, but it
is as certain that we *can* be saved. It is the office
work of Christ to save ; it is his pleasure to save ;
it is his determination to save. He came from
heaven to earth to seek and to save that which was
lost. There is not a single individual here to-day
but Christ can save. Doutless, there is not one
who has gone too *far* to be saved; not one who is
too *wicked* to be saved ; not one who has lived in
this world of sin too *long* to be saved. There may,
indeed, be some persons laboring under impressions that they are so. They may think it now
too late to be saved. The devil tells sinners, when
young, it is too soon for them to begin to be saved ;
that they may go on in sin until they become old ;
and now when they are old, he tells them it is too
late to be saved; but O, believe him not. As long
as Christ is in heaven, and you are upon the earth,
it is possible for you to be saved.

"Your case is bad, yet it is not hopeless. Do
not say with wicked Cain, 'My punishment is

greater than I can bear;' or, 'My sins are too great to be forgiven.' Come to the throne of grace this day, under the impression that you *must* and *may* be saved. God can save you. Christ can redeem you; the Holy Spirit can sanctify you. He can take the stony heart out of your flesh, and give you an heart of flesh. He can give you the spirit of prayer. He can give you a penitent, contrite heart. He can pardon your sins. He can receive you graciously, and it is possible for you to experience all this on earth, and you *must* experience it on earth, or you *must* be lost. If you can be saved, if there is provision for sinners, and for the chief of sinners, why *may you* not be saved? This is the

"*Third* idea, to which your attention is called.

"After all your ingratitude, unbelief, impenitence, and hardness of heart, *you may* be saved. Will you not seriously think of this? Will you not, fellow-sinners, meditate and pray, till your hearts are filled with gratitude to God for telling you, in his holy word, that it is possible you may be saved? You *may* be saved, as assuredly as you hear me this day. You may be saved, as assuredly as you are sinners. Hear what Jehovah says: 'As I live, saith the Lord God, I have no pleasure in the death of the wicked.' And we find Peter, when preaching from the same text, saying, 'He willeth not the death of the sinner, but rather that he should repent, that he may live.'

"But you are not to suppose, fellow-men, that you *may* be saved, if you continue in your sins. No; if you live and die under the *power* of sin, you *cannot* be saved. If you believe not on the Lord Jesus Christ, you *may* not be saved; you *will* be lost. 'Except ye repent, ye shall all likewise perish

6

"Can you select any one person of your acquaintance, of whom it is said, in any part of the Bible, that *he may* not be saved? Yet it is not because a person prays, that he is to be saved. For if it be asked, In whose name do you pray? should you answer, For my own soul's sake let me be saved, that would not do. No name can prevail in heaven but the name of Christ, and through Christ God has promised to sanctify the soul; for he hath promised that he will receive into heaven all those that are believers in Christ Jesus. Christ has opened the gates of heaven for all true believers. May you feel all this, and be enabled to say, in the language of the Old Testament, 'Into thy hands I commit my spirit,' and also to say, from your hearts, as it is written in the New Testament, 'Lord, if thou wilt, thou canst make me clean.'

"*Lastly.* I ask you now seriously, fellow-sinner, whether you are really *willing* to be saved. You *must*, you *can*, you *may* be saved; then, I ask you, whether you *will* be saved? I do not ask you whether you need salvation; you *do* need it. I do not ask you whether you can save yourself; you cannot save yourself. But I ask you, *will* you be saved? I cannot save you; Christians cannot save you: saints and angels in heaven cannot save you; but the Lord Jesus Christ can, and with him I leave you, not, however, without once more reminding you, as I close this short discourse, that we shall each of us be personally *saved* in *heaven*, or personally *lost* in *hell*.

"Sinners the voice of God regard,
'Tis mercy speaks to-day;
He calls you by his sovereign word,
From sin's destructive way.

"Your way is dark and leads to hell,
  Why will you persevere;
Can you in endless torments dwell,
  Shut up in black despair?

"Why will you in the crooked paths
  Of sin and folly go?
In pain you travel all your days,
  To reap immortal woe!

"But he that turns to God shall live,
  Through his abounding grace;
His mercy will the guilt forgive,
  Of those that seek his face.

"You are taught by this subject, reader, that you are not excluded from Christ and life by the greatness of your sins; but if you perish, it must be from another cause: it must be on account of your wilful unbelief, in not accepting of Jesus Christ as your Saviour. Come, then, you that have been ringleaders in vice, come now, take the lead, and show others the way to Jesus Christ; harlots, publicans, thieves, blasphemers, and murderers, if such be among you, there is salvation even for you, if you will but believe. O, how astonishing is the love of God discovered in this way! this way of life through his only Son."

THE CASE OF SEAMEN.

Extracts from a sermon preached by Rev. J. P. K. Henshaw, Balt.

"THE very nature of their occupation cuts them off from the ordinary means of grace and religious improvement, during a great portion of their lives. It is estimated that seamen are on shore not more than one-fourth of their time; consequently, the remainder is spent upon the bosom of the deep. They are, during three-fourths of their time, separated from home and kindred—from all that is improving and refining in domestic life—and, what is more lamentable, from all the public and social means of grace. To them no holy Sabbath marks the revolution of the week, by its welcome offer of repose for the body and instruction for the soul. They are never called to bend the knee in common prayer to our common Father in heaven, nor to unite their voices in the social hymn of praise. No ambassador of peace proclaims in their ears the joyful tidings of redeeming love. No sacramental table, with its holy and inviting symbols, is spread before them, to remind them of the pains and agonies of Him who was crucified for their sins, and of the rich spiritual feast which he has provided for their souls. They may, indeed, 'see the works of the Lord, and his wonders in the deep;'—they may behold the heavens he has made, the moon and the stars which he has ordained;—they may hear his threatenings in the tempest and the thunder, and perceive his mercy in their deliverance from perils; and, if possessed of the volume of his word, they may cast their eye over its sacred pages; but alas! if their minds are not-stored with religious sentiments, and they have not the eye of faith, all will be a wide and unmeaning blank that will impart no instruction, and excite no proper feelings in their hearts:—'They regard not the works of the Lord, nor consider the operations of his hands.' If we find that, on land, where the means of grace abound,—where men have 'line upon line, and precept upon precept,—here a little and there a little.' so few are truly devoted to God, and active in religion,—it would be like looking for impossibilities, and supposing seamen to be more than human, to expect that their minds would be stored with Christian knowledge, and their actions governed by Christian precepts, under the circumstances of destitution in which they are placed.

"Till within a few years past, an entire indifference and apathy on this subject prevailed. The poor seamen arrived on our shores, and, so far from being surrounded by the agents of benevolence and friends of religion, who desire to promote their temporal and eternal welfare, they were seized by harpies, dragged to the haunts of dissipation and vice, and, like the poor man who fell among thieves, 'stripped, wounded, and left half dead;' and the friends of humanity and religion, as if utterly forgetful of their duties, like the priest and Levite, in the parable, left them to the mercy of their tormentors, 'and passed by on the other side!'

"Can we wonder, then, at the low state of religion and morals among seamen, when no man cared for their souls? when no counsellors appeared to instruct them in the knowledge of God, and no kind friends took them by the hand to lead them in the way of life? Must not a part of the guilt be laid at our doors? Have they not a strong claim to our compassion and benevolence, grounded upon our former insensibility to their misery, and neglect of their best interests? Is it not time that we begin in earnest to act the part of the good Samaritan?"

OBLIGATIONS TO SEAMEN.

"What Christian man does not long for the time when there shall be no farther displays of naval skill, and martial valor—when the brave and generous spirits of whom I am speaking, baptized with the spirit of the Gospel, will carry the news of salvation with them in all their voyages, and go, as swift messengers, to corrupt and idolatrous nations, bearing the joyful tidings of peace with God, and good-will to all mankind!

"To seamen we are indebted for many of our comforts, and almost all of our luxuries. They commit themselves to the perils of the deep, brave the storm and the tempest, and visit foreign climes, for the purpose of supplying delicacies for our tables, ornaments for our persons, books for our libraries, and decorations for our dwellings. When feasting upon imported luxuries; when clothed in purple or fine linen; when admiring your splendid and finely-wrought articles of furniture; or enriching your minds with the treasures of foreign genius and science; think of the claims of the sailor, by whose toil and exposure these things have been procured for you. Let the merchant, especially, reflect upon the heavy debt of gratitude he owes. When counting the wealth in his coffers, when surveying his store-houses, filled with the valuable productions of other countries,—when living in ease, affluence, and splendor,—let him call to mind, that, under a gracious Providence, he is chiefly indebted for all his possessions and comforts, to the sweat and toil of the hardy seamen, who have submitted to a temporary banishment from their native land, with all its privileges and comforts, from Sabbaths and sanctuaries and home; and let him ask, what return he can make for the labors and sacrifices to which they have submitted in his service? . Ah! where is our boasted patriotism, if we make no acknowledgments to those who have been the supporters and defenders of our country's rights and liberties? Where are our principles of justice and honor, if we offer no return of benefits to those who have so largely contributed to our prosperity and wealth? Have we even the virtue of the degraded and vicious publicans, if we do not good to those who have done good to us?"

MEANS OF GRACE.

The same means of grace that serve as channels through which light and consolation are poured into the souls of other men, must be extended to our seafaring brethren, if we hope to see them made partakers of the salvation which is in Christ Jesus. They must have the word of life and other books of religious instruction put into their hands. Not a ship should sail from a Christian port without a supply of Bibles and religious tracts. In the hours of loneliness and weariness incident to a voyage, the most negligent and hardened might be led to take up a tract and read it, from motives of curiosity or amusement, or for want of other employment. And that tract, before contemned and ridiculed, might be the instrument, in the hands of the Holy Spirit, of arresting the attention of the sinner—of opening his mind to perceive the realities of an eternal world, and leading him, as a trembling penitent, to the foot of the cross. There are times in every seaman's life, when, by the force of outward circumstances, he must be led to reflect on God, the soul, and eternity. "Those men that go down to the sea in ships, and do business in great waters, see the works of the Lord, and

his wonders in the deep." When looking abroad
upon the wide and boundless expanse of the ocean,
or gazing at the spangled firmament ; when the
surrounding calm at once invites and compels to
reflection, what rays of light and lessons of wisdom would the volume of revelation shed upon
the otherwise blank and unintelligible book of
nature ?   How would the perusal of his Bible,
under circumstances like these, inspire the sail-
or's mind with lofty conceptions of the character
of Him who formed all the wonders upon which
his eye had gazed; and cause his heart to bow
with reverence and devotion before that Almighty
being, " who spread out the heavens as a curtain,
and laid the foundations of the earth ; whose paths
are in the mighty waters, and whose footsteps are
not known ?" ·

And when the calm has passed away, when the
hemisphere is black with clouds ; when the tempest rages with all its fury, and the agitated sea
tosses her waves on high, when the guilty mariner
hears in every blast the threatenings of an angry
Judge, and in the horror of anticipated death,
asks, " ' What must I do to be saved ?' how can I
be prepared to meet my God ?". O where can he
find a solution of his doubts and an answer to his
inquiries, but in the Bible ?   That blessed volume
tells him of one who " delivereth from the wrath
to come," directs him to " believe in the Lord
Jesus Christ and he shall be saved !"   Those to
whom the Bible is precious, who have made it the
man of their counsel, who have an experimental
knowledge of its saving truths, may be calm and
collected, even amidst the terrors of such a scene.
They know in whom they have believed, and have
cast their anchor of hope within the vail, fast by

the throne of God. And therefore, while all is noisy and tempestuous without, all is peaceful and tranquil within; and amidst the rattling of the shrouds, the creaking of the masts, and the howling of the storm, they can lift up their mild and submissive countenances to the heavens, and perhaps with tremulous but yet joyful voices sing,

> "The God that rules on high,
>   And thunders when he please, .
> That rides upon the stormy sky
>   And manages the seas:—

> "This awful God is ours,
>   Our Father, and our love;
> · He shall send down his heavenly powers
>   To carry us above."
>
> *Sailor's Magazine*

A BLASPHEMER CONVERTED.

" THE following interesting anecdote was related by a person who keeps a boarding-house in Liverpool, England. A Scotch seaman, who was, as expressed by his shipmates, a horrid blasphemer, on his late passage home from the Indies, wanting something out of the forecastle, was groping for it, when he clapped his hand on a book which one of the men had been reading in his watch below; curiosity induced him to examine its contents. It was a Testament; he opened it, and with surprise and attention read the denouncement of God's anger against wicked blasphemers. The exact words the friend could not recollect, but they certainly were applied with the power of the Holy Spirit. From that time a striking and decided change has occurred in his habits and character, for he has forsaken his bad companions, and broken off all evil practices. He who was before a bold and dauntless swearer, is now found conversing with his shipmates about spiritual and eternal truths :—he whose only happiness appeared to be in ale-houses, brothels, &c., is now to be found a consistent attendant at the prayer-meetings and house of God. The testimony of those who witnessed this change of character is a strong conviction of the reality of the change.

"Still another. A sailor, after one of the prayer-meetings in Liverpool, was observed much dejected : he addressed one of the friends, saying, 'I have heard your prayers for mercy upon sailors, and you have encouraged us to pray, and hope for mercy ; but alas ! I am in the gall of bitterness and in the bonds of iniquity. When I think of eternity, I dread the thought of being banished from the Almighty, and from happiness, into "outer darkness"; this distresses me beyond expression.' He was asked what caused these thoughts. He said, 'he was first invited to the meetings by a shipmate ; for some time he was very indifferent about what was going forward, or what he heard, but he still attended ; at length his mind *gave way ;* if there was truth in these things he was a poor lost soul ; his heart began to melt, and to force him to pray for forgiveness of his sins ; he soon forsook his drunken habits, and waited pleading at mercy's door ; but; alas ! he feared, and his conscience accused him of sinning against the Holy Ghost.' The poor fellow was encouraged to continue to pray, as these thoughts were temptations from the evil one ; for if the Lord had not thoughts of mercy, He would not by his

Spirit have alarmed him to flee from the wrath to
come, and assisted him by his grace to forsake
his evil companions and drunken habits. He felt
encouraged to persevere'; and now he is thanking
God for removing guilt from his conscience, and
assisting him to enjoy fellowship with his people.

Sailor's Magazine.

THE STRANGER'S BURYING PLACE.

" *April* 12th. Arose early on Saturday morning, and went to Whampoa. Spent part of the
afternoon on French Island, where multitudes of
natives and foreigners await the morning of the
resurrection. Here are three groups of strangers,
occupying different places, though out a short distance apart. The two most contiguous to the
present anchorage are of a recent date, and principally consist of Americans and English. The
tombs of the other are inscribed in different lan-
guages, and refer you, with a few exceptions, to
the past century. The majority were cut off in
the vigor of youth, and very many without a moment's warning Probably the comparative number of drowned is without a parallel in any ceme-
tery ; and of all this number there. are very few,
if any, who had passed the morning of life. What
a solemn admonition to thoughtless youth. It is
surprising that those who fall from the ships, however expert they may be at swimming, and even
accustomed to exercise in this very river, seldom
arise to the surface, or are rescued from the grasp
of death. Many a mound is pointed out where
sleep the bodies of those who were healthy, gay,
and unapprehensive of their change the very mo-

ment before their deathful plunge. In the midst
of cheerful conversation there was an abrupt pause
a sudden dash, and an awful eternity.—*Mr. Abeel'
Journal at Canton.*

_____   (

THE FRAILTY OF MAN.

"Lord, what is man—his pride—his pomp—his glory?"

"How frail is man!—a sail, a little bark,,
   Combats the raging of the mighty sea ;
And when the sky with awful clouds is dark,
   Father of lights, we lift each voice to thee.

"Then hear us from the sounding billow's crest,
   Uplifted to the lightnings of the sky,
By all the fury of the tempest press'd—
   Benignant Father, hear our humble cry.

"To the wild wave our little vessel reels—
   The dreary fires have lit the sullen main:
And the proud heart, reft of its greatness, feels
   That all but Thou must stretch the hand in vain.

"The thunder shakes the rain-drop from the clouds,—
   The creaking mast bends to the raging gale,
That in loud murmurs whistles through the shrouds—
   God of the storm !—what can a worm avail?

"Wild on the wind the seaman's shouts arise—
   The petrel shrieks amid the snowy spray,
Rent by the gale the bursting canvas flies ;—
   God of the thunder—speed the storm away.

"Thou see'st the mother rushing in despair
   To the damp decks, the infant at her breast,
Wild is her eye, and loose her moistened hair ;—
   Friend of the wretched—pity the distress'd.   ∵

"Thou see'st the sons support their fathers' head,
   Death! bitter death, has dimm'd affection's eye ;
Thou hear'st their groans, thou see'st the tears they shed ;
   Smile, God of Nature, from the murky sky.

Smile in the sun's beams, Parent of the seas!
God of the whirlwind, with thy soothing breath,
Check the wild tempest, and the howling breeze;-
Father—'tis thine to give us life or death.
Sailor's Magazine

VICE PROGRESSIVE.

Extract from a sermon lately delivered in New York, by the *Rev. J. P. Thompson*, occasioned by the ignominious death of a young man in New Haven, where Mr. T. was formerly settled in the pastoral office.

"SOME ten years ago he was a pupil in the Sabbath school in which I was then a teacher. He was a well-behaved youth; neither profane, idle, nor vicious; and as he grew up to manhood, he acquired a character for industry and sobriety. Occasionally, indeed, he fell into loose company, but was soon reclaimed by parental kindness and authority, so that till he became of age, he was never openly vicious, and seldom absent from his father's house at unreasonable hours. In short, his general deportment at this period would have compared favorably with that of the youth in any well-regulated household. About four years ago, when nineteen years of age, he began to attend on my ministry, and in the course of a few months, having entertained hope in Christ, he made a public profession of religion. Well do I remember my first conversation with him on that subject,— and the serious and satisfactory narration which he then gave of his religious experience. He joined the church in June, 1843, and month after month came to the table of the Lord: he doubtless thought that he was truly converted, and he

7

led for some time a life of apparent devotion. In about a year, however, it was noticed that he was irregular in his attendance on public worship, and painful rumors of his delinquency reached the ears of his brethren; who could not watch over him strictly on account of the distance at which he lived. Having become of age, he had left his father's house and was employed upon the railroad near by. Here he fell in with wicked companions; some of whom were already steeped in vice. He began to neglect his Bible and his customary scenes of devotion, and to suspect, what was probably the fact, that his religion had been more a matter of excitement than of principle. Away from Christian influences, surrounded by profane and licentious companions, he gradually became profane and licentious himself. These facts being ascertained by the church, every effort was made to induce him to return to his duty;—but whether through shame, or from a premature hardening in guilt, he refused to hold any communication with the church, or to make any promise of amendment, and was therefore excommunicated.

" It seems difficult to account for this sudden fall; but it occurred substantially as follows :—Returning from work, one evening, he casually stopped for a moment by a house of evil resort, which his companions, who were familiar with the place, proposed that he should go in with them. At first he hesitated, but curiosity on the one hand, and ridicule on the other, overcame his scruples. He went, however, as a mere spectator; and as he saw at once the grossest forms of vice, he soon left the place in disgust, thinking that he would never enter it again. But, alas! he knew not his own weakness. He had dallied with temptation. Had he

remembered that lesson of the Sabbath School,
My son, if sinners entice thee, consent thou not, he
would have stopped his ears against his tempt-
ers, and have escaped for his life. But no; he
would venture a little farther; he would see for
himself—confident of self-control. And what was
the result? While he was disgusted he was in-
flamed. He had looked in at the gate of hell and
had taken fire before he could retreat. What he
saw was an exhibition of human passions, and *he*
had passions that could revel in just such scenes.
' Can a man take fire in his bosom, and his clothes
not be burned? Can one go upon hot coals, and
his feet not be burned?' So it was with that
young man. He came away shocked in his moral
sense, but excited in his passions; and he went
again to that den of infamy, of his own accord. In
consenting to go there, even from curiosity, he
broke away from the most powerful restraints, and
he was obliged, at the first, to plunge deep into the
abyss, to quench the light of truth and grace that
had burned within him from his earliest years.
His parents sought him, again and again, but obtained from him only promises of amendment,
which were never kept.

" He was cut off from the church in September,
1844. Two weeks ago to-day I knelt in that mur-
derer's cell, in company with his parents, sister
and brother, who had come for their last interview
with him on earth. That narrow cell was more
solemn than the grave itself. Two weeks ago to-
morrow I saw the youth who had once been of my
spiritual flock, upon the scaffold. It was an awful
scene; it haunts me in my sleep, my heart sick-
ens at the remembrance of it, and I shudder to
speak of what I hardly dared to look upon.

" About a hundred persons, principally civil and military officers, are assembled in the yard of the prison, which is carefully screened from all without. The clear blue sky is overhead, the bright sun is shining, but the air seems stifled, and men breathe heavily and slow.

" Upon a scaffold some ten feet high stands the youthful criminal, in the habiliments of death. He makes a brief address, he hears a parting prayer, he bids adieu to those around, the knot is tied, the face, is covered: the spring is touched—the trap falls—and all is ended. No, all is not ended : but we must leave him with his Judge."

In the exhortation with which the preacher concluded his discourse, he thus feelingly addresses the young :

" I know your dangers, for my own youth was spent in a great city, and I have sailed till my head was dizzy on the outer edge of that whirlpool, where some of you may soon be struggling for your very life. Alas! the *dead* are there ; and I come to you charged with a message from the dead. Do you say that this case is peculiar ? I admit it. But .*how* is it peculiar ? Are you the son of pious parents ? So was he. Have you been trained in a Sabbath School ? So was he. More than this ; he had thought that he was a Christian. The case is peculiar in that it shows that every moral barrier may be overleaped by lust; it warns every one who thinketh he standeth to take heed lest he fall.

" Oh! that you could have heard the warning of that wretched young man, from the scaffold. ' You know,' said he, ' how I was brought up. I had the best instructions a Christian father could give. O if I had followed them, I should have been over yon mountain, in my dear father's home. But temptation led me astray, and I have come to this. I hope now, as I leave this world, my voice will warn all young men. Our desires and passions are so strong, that it requires very little to lead us astray. I want to urge it upon all young men never to take the first step in such a career as mine. When the first step is taken in the paths of sin, it is difficult to stop.' *His* 'first step' was a desperate leap, from which he could not recover ; yours may be less marked, a sliding, as it were, down an inclined plane. I warn you of it; I warn you against idleness, the parent of vice, the parent of those evil imaginings that make the soul the cage of unclean birds. I warn you against evil books, however fascinating ; against company, however gay and tempting. 'Enter not into the path of the wicked, and go not in the way of evil men ; avoid it, pass not by it, turn from it, and pass away.' I warn you against vain amusements and places of evil resort; against the theatre, the ball-room, the drinking club, the gaming table. I warn you of the wiles of her who lieth in wait at the corners of the streets. 'Let not thine heart incline to her ways; go not astray in her paths. For she hath cast down many wounded, yea many strong men have been slain by her.' I warn you to cleave to God's testimonies, and walk in his ways. As I stood beneath t' at scaffold, the painful thought crossed my min , Has any omission of duty on my part towards this young man contributed in any manner to his end ? I resolved, that at least no other youth under my ministry should come to such an end unwarned by me. And I am here to-night to fulfil that vow, to discharge my soul of its heavy responsibility to you, *young men.*

I warn you, therefore, in his name; I warn you by the memory of that dreadful scene; I warn you before God, MOST HIGH—*your* JUDGE and *mine* And if there be a deeper note of warning still, I will be silent, that it may come to you from the *chambers of the dead*—from the ABYSS OF WOE."

THE AGED SAILOR ENTERING THE HARBOR.

" THE events of our early years, while passing, seem to us of little importance, further than concerns our own childish interests. It is the play-day of our existence, and the due estimation of its importance is reserved for after years. In mature age we often meet with scenes which transport us back to childhood, and develop the consequences of events apparently so trivial. The truth of these remarks will be illustrated by the narrative I am about to give of an aged sailor.

" When a school-boy, I used to pass his house on my way to the place of instruction. He lived about midway between my father's dwelling and the school-house, and on a cold winter morning I frequently called to warm my chilled fingers. Whenever my sailor friend was at home, he gave me a welcome reception, and entertained my wondering fancy with his tales of the sea. I became quite attached to him, and the attachment was mutual. In the lapse of years, the school-boy became a clergyman, and the sailor became old and weather-beaten. A dissipated life, with the storms of the ocean, and an occasional shipwreck had broken down his hardy constitution, and now, no

longer 'seaworthy,' he was cast, poor and miserable, upon the land, like a thing shattered and driv-
en ashore by the tempest. In consequence of his
wicked life and infirmities, he was abandoned by
his old employers, and came home on foot, without
money, and almost without clothing. On his arrival, he was so filthy in his appearance that none
desired his society; and he wandered about in a
kind of partial derangement, calling aloud on the
inhabitants as he passed their dwellings, at dead
of night, to awake and repent. Soon after this
time, his old friend the school-boy returned from
a missionary tour, to spend a few days in his native town. He was told that the old Captain was
confined chiefly to his bed, in great distress of
mind, despairing of salvation. The scenes of my
chilhood burst afresh upon me—the winter's fire,
my sailor friend, and his enchanting tales of the
sea. I went immediately to see him. He lay in
a apartment indicating poverty and distress, but
he heeded no longer external circumstances; he
was pondering the loss of his soul. The clergyman of the parish, and some Christians, had told
him, *unscripturally*, that his life had been such
that probably no mercy remianed for him. I
found him believing their erroneous counsel, and
tossing in the agonies of despair. 'Oh,' said he,
'I am a poor, old, weather-beaten sailor, tossing
about in the storm, and I can't find a harbor.
There is no mercy for such an old sinner.' 'Don't
say that,' I replied: 'how do you know?' and I
took down his old canvas-covered Bible, and began
to read of Paul, of Peter, of David, and of the
great mercies of the Lord to the chief of sinners.
'How?' said he, 'do you say I can be saved?'
'Yes, if you come to Christ, for he is able and

willing to save the chief of sinners, if they repent and believe.' 'You are the first man that told me that,' he exclaimed : ' the first man that told me I could be saved.' While a beam of hope lighted up his dejected visage, I assured him that it was not too late for the returning prodigal. He believed my testimony, and with all the frankness and ardor characteristic of his profession, began to confess his sins, and lift up his prayer to Him, who walked upon the waves, and quieted the stormy sea. In this state of mind, I left him, and soon called to see him again. He was still in the dark, but anxiously striving for entrance at the strait gate. I described in a simple manner the path of life; directed him to the abundant consolations for the penitent; commended him to God, and was about to retire, when he stopped me. ' How mysterious it is!' he said: 'a little while ago you was a school-boy, and stopped to warm your hands at my fire : I little thought then, that you would be a minister, and come here to show a poor old sinner how to be saved. I wonder how you can condescend to visit such a miserable old creature.' His thankfulness was affecting from its fulness and simplicity; and I stole away, lest I should be tempted to receive the praise which belongeth to God alone.

"On my third visit, I found the old mariner full of joy. He had found the harbor. The Great Pilot had appeared, and conducted his weather-beaten bark into the port of peace. He lived but a short time, and departed with the full assurance of leaving a stormy ocean, for the haven of eternal rest. I love to dwell on the story of his life, and conversion, and happy exit. Rich was the grace bestowed in the hour of need ; and fully was illustrated the truth, that the chief of sinners may be saved. Hallowed now are those scenes of my childhood. I can never forget the school-boy, the winter fire, and my sailor friend."

Sailor's Mag.   M.

THERE'S HOPE FOR THEE.

A Sailor's Hymn.

" Blest be that voice, now heard afar,
    O'er the dark, rolling sea,
That whispers to the hardy tar,
    ' Sailor, there's hope for thee!'

" Blest be that pure, that Christian love,
    That boundless charity,
Which bears the olive like the dove,
    Brave, generous tar, for thee.

" Blest be those lips, in accents mild,
    From sordid motives free,
That first proclaimed to Ocean's child,
    ' Sailor, there's hope for thee.'

" Long hadst thou rode the foamy wave,
    From sin nor danger free,
Till mercy stretch'd her arm to save-
    To save, brave sailor, thee.

Sailor's Magazine.

BETHEL SUMMARIES.

Communicated by Rev. H. Chase, Seamen's Preacher.

" A seaman called on me, and gave the following account of the conversion of two officers on board the ship ———; himself. and the son of captain J.

"Mr. H said he was twenty-five years old, and had followed the sea fourteen years. He was very wild and unsteady, and a devoted servant of sin, previous to his late serious impressions. After he became an officer, he was very harsh and cruel to his men, and sometimes his conduct was even that of a tyrant. At one time he had carried his tyranny to such lengths during a voyage, that he was obliged to run away as soon as he got in port for fear of a process at law. He continued in a course of sin and dissipation, not however without some checks of conscience, till he attended a Bethel meeting, last August, on board the Empress, when his mind became seriously impressed, by the prayers and exhortations during the meeting. He saw, in a manner that he had never seen before, that he was a sinner on the way to ruin; and he determined on the spot that he would lead a new life. He soon after shipped on board the ship ——, captain J., bound to ——. During the outward-bound passage, he endeavored to put his resolution in practice, but found no peace of mind. While lying in ——, the second mate, (son of captain J.) a young man about nineteen years of age, and who had been under serious impressions for some time, invited him one evening to go with him to meeting, but he declined; and after spending a short time on shore, he came on board at an early hour, and retired to his state-room. Here he remained some time, meditating on his miserable condition, and his awful prospects for futurity. At length the second mate returned from meeting, and entered the state-room in the greatest agony of mind, crying, 'Oh, my Saviour, have mercy on me, a miserable sinner. Oh Lord, forgive my sins. Oh, I feel the Lord's displeasure

upon me, but my blessed Saviour died for me.'
These exclamations and petitions were mingled
with many a bitter groan. This produced a powerful impression on the mind of Mr. H., and to use
his own language, it went to his heart. And
though he had not as yet experienced the grace
of God, and knew little of the way of salvation, he
endeavored to give him some comfort, by telling
him to seek the Lord, for he had frequently heard
Christians say, that if we sought the Lord with all
our hearts we should find him. The second mate
then went to his own state-room, and left Mr. H.
to weep and pray over his own miserable condition. At length Mr. H , after many a melancholy
reflection, sunk into an unsound and fitful slumber. By and by Mr. J. rushed again into his
state-room, in the greatest ecstasy, saying, ' Oh!
Mr. H., I have found the Lord,—Oh, I have found
my dear Saviour:—Glory to God, he has had
mercy upon me!'

" Thus the Lord was graciously pleased to set
the soul of this young man at liberty, and give
him that peace which passeth understanding.

" Mr. H. attended the meetings several times
while they were at ———, and had the prayers
of God's people in his behalf, but he obtained no
comfort. He felt himself a vile and wicked sinner, and seemed to think he was abandoned both
by God and man. He thought all had deserted
him, and turned against him, and there was no
comfort for him, either from heaven or earth. He
could sleep but little, and that little was interrupted by frightful dreams. Thus was the Lord
humbling his proud heart, and preparing him for
the rich displays of divine grace. One thing in
particular deserves to be mentioned, which took

place while they were lying in ——, which is much to the credit of the captain. He knew what was going on with his officers, and no doubt encouraged them to seek the Lord. One Sabbath morning Mr. H. ordered the men to get the buckets, to wash off the decks. But while he gave the order, he felt as if his heart would sink; he hesitated; he knew that it was the holy Sabbath of the Lord; and he would rather make any sacrifice than violate the Lord's day. However, he knew what was his duty as first officer, according to the common usage on board a ship; and he proceeded, with an aching heart, to perform it. At this moment the captain came on deck. 'Mr. H.,' said he, ' the decks were washed off last night, were they not?' 'Yes, sir,' was the reply. ' Oh, well, it is not necessary to wash them now, they are clean enough.' Mr. H. felt that a load was removed from him, and with a light heart he ordered the buckets put away.

"While he was in this painful state of mind, the ship sailed for New York. He generally spent his watch below in reading his Bible, and hymns, and praying to God for mercy upon his soul. The day before they arrived, during his forenoon watch, he was lying in his berth · reading the Scriptures, and praying that he might have something to comfort his mind, and direct him in the right way. In the course of his reading, he came to the 11th chapter and 24th verse of Mark: ' Therefore I say unto you, what things soever ye desire, when ye pray, believe that ye receive them, and ye shall have them.' Immediately it struck his mind, that though he had often prayed, he had not prayed in faith; he had not believed in Jesus Christ with a living faith; he had not given up his heart to the Lord. He started from his berth immediately, threw himself upon his knees before his Saviour, and lifted up his heart in prayer to God. The Lord helped him; he was enabled to cast himself upon the mercy of God, and Jesús spoke peace to his soul. He felt the burden removed from his heart, and then for the first time rejoiced in the God of his salvation."

REV. MR. ABEEL'S JOURNAL AT SEA.

" *Sabbath, Nov.* 1, 1829.—The most delightful day since we left our native land. Wind and weather favorable. Sick from the motion of the vessel, but much improved, and what is far more important, public worship celebrated. This morning our cabin was consecrated to the service of God. It was thought the most appropriate place in the ship. The behavior of those present was becoming, their attention riveted. They were addressed familiarly on the talents which had been intrusted to them, the obligations under which they are placed, the judgment to which they are destined, · and the consequences of profitably employing, or criminally neglecting, their advantages. In the afternoon, conversation with some of the young men, on the importance of personal religion. It was gratifying to see sailors perusing tracts after service, while in some instances, others would be looking over their shoulders, either reading, or listening and spelling.

" *Thursday, Nov.* 20, 1829.—This afternoon I summoned up resolution, and made a visit in the forecastle. I did apprehend harsh treatment from some, who have openly and unblushingly blasphemed

the name of God in my presence. One of them
had been indisposed for some time, and I conceived
it a favorable opportunity of conversing with him
on the great subject, which he neglected in health,
and to which God's afflictive hand, in an especial
manner, directed his attention. As I entered his
apartment, my cars were assailed with oaths, and
instead of finding the sick man in a serious mood,
I soon ascertained that they proceeded from his
lips. Pale, emaciated, and enfeebled by disease, I
was shocked at his insensibility and hardihood, and
immediately endeavored to convince him of his
guilt and danger. I remained probably an hour
conversing with him, and intentionally, though
without a direct reference, to those who mingled
with us   Silence, and as far as I can judge, a conviction of the truth, were the consequence.

" *Nov.* 27th.—To-day is my ordinary visit to the
apartment of the sick ; two or three of the sailors
came in, and remained with us some time. I
addressed them with such remarks and questions as
I thought appropriate. They were exceedingly
wicked, as I had witnessed in their conversation
and conduct, but appeared open to conviction, and
impressed with the remarks and exhortations.
Though in many instances greatly depraved, they
are by no means destitute of feeling, and when
addressed with earnestness and solemnity, are can-
did in acknowledgments of guilt. and for the time,
at least, apparently convinced of the need of refor-
mation.

" *Nov.* 30.—Yesterday we enjoyed our estab-
lished privilege at morning and afternoon service.
The crew were generally present, and especially in
the afternoon. Never since we commenced preaching. did I witness such fixed attention ; and never

since we sailed, has the Sabbath been so well observed. To-day I received a note from one of the sailors, desiring an interview, with a special reference to religious information. As it bore the evident marks of sincerity, it afforded more pleasure than any object my eyes had seen during the passage. In the evening, I saw the young man, by whom it was signed, walking the decks alone. When he saw me approaching, he waited; and when I addressed him, unhesitatingly entered into conversation. He mentioned that his attention had been previously directed to religion, by a tract which he read during the last voyage; but as he could find none disposed to converse on serious subjects, but on the other hand, as there was a disposition prevalent among them to ridicule religion, and deride its adherents, he became indifferent to his best interest, and, on his return, yielded to the temptations which beset the homeless mariner. Within the last week, his convictions have revived. He feels the necessity of religion, but finds his heart a stone. He inquired with anxiety, whether there was a class of human beings for whom there was no salvation. His sins, and particularly the aggravated guilt of resisting the Holy Spirit and stifling strong convictions, probably suggested the idea.

"The more I converse with seamen, the more I am impressed with the indispensable necessity of having a revolution in their boarding system on shore. The evil is deprecated not only by the officers, but also by the deluded sailors, when calm reflection succeeds the hours of revelry passed in these haunts of vice. They are the very gates of destruction standing open. While they afford to infernal spirits, a free access to the heart of the infatuated seaman, they conduct their unguarded captive by a short passage to hell. Here those reflections that might lead to repentance, are debarred from the mind; or, if entertained, effectually expelled. This influence has been exerted upon the poor young man, whose heart is now alive to remorse : he continued serious, however, and subsequently gave evidence of piety."

"SHE BEING DEAD, YET SPEAKETH."

In presenting the first annual report of the Female Bethel Society of Newburyport, we have to record the death of one of its most valued members (Miss Frances Davenport;) one, whose warmest sympathies were enlisted in the cause, and whose active co-operation gave an efficiency to this society, such as is seldom the result of individual effort. Long after disease had marked her for its victim, and when unable, through weakness, to converse on other subjects, her interest in the sailor was unabated, and her last efforts were made in his behalf. Noticing from the window of her room, on a pleasant Sabbath morning, a company of sailors, she at once availed herself of the opportunity to distribute among them some tracts which she had previously selected. In attempting to throw them from the window, one was taken by the wind, and carried into an adjoining field ; and as she stood anxiously watching its fate, she caught the eye of one of the company, who, observing her emaciated appearance, seemed eager to possess the treasure, which she had been at so much pains to bestow, and losing no time, he leaped over the fence, and soon made it his own. Her thoughts followed that sailor, and, in alluding to the circumstance afterwards, she expressed the hope, that it might prove the means of his salvation. Let the motto, then, which we would inscribe to her memory, serve as a memorial for future years, from which to date our onward progress; thus borrowed from eternity, the hallowed fire, with which to animate our zeal and enkindle our offerings. Our own souls being lighted at the altar, we may light the lamp of many a weary traveller over the pathless ocean, who, amidst the shoals and quicksands, has none to guide his little bark, or point him to the port of safety. "That unseen eye, which watches over the fall of the sparrow, with far more scrutinizing gaze, is fixed upon the homeless mariner; and, as the threatening wave is lifted, ready to devour, the voice of supplication reaches his ear, and the raging tempest ceases :—or the heavenly mandate has perhaps extended farther than the depth of the ocean, breaking the slumbers of the soul, and awakening it from its fatal repose. Resting now, upon the arms of Omnipotence, he heeds not the rolling billow, for the footsteps of his Saviour are there; and, like Peter, in all the ardor of attachment, he is ready to mount the surge, if he might discern a distant approach. Truly, "His way is in the sea, his path in the deep waters." "In the fourth watch of the night, Jesus came, walking upon the water:" so ready was he to administer to the relief and comfort of his disciples, and so ready is he now to answer the prayers of his people if offered to him in sincerity Leaning then upon Almighty strength. and planting one foot upon the promises, what may not this infant society

8*

accomplish? How many of the sons of the ocean.
would throng the temple gates of Zion ? " bringing
their silver and their gold with them, as an offer-
ing unto the Lord, as a thank-offering to his Holy
Name."

SAILOR'S HYMN.

" Toss'd upon life's raging billow,
    Sweet it is, O Lord, to know
Thou didst press a sailor's pillow,
    And canst feel a sailor's woe.
Never slumbering, never sleeping,
    Though the night be dark and drear,
Thou the faithful watch art keeping,
    ' All, all's well,' thy constant cheer.

" And though loud the wind is howling,
    Fierce though flash the lightnings red ;
Darkly through the storm—clouds scowling
    O'er the sailor's anxious head :—
Thou canst calm the raging ocean,
    All its noise and tumult still !
Hush the tempest's wild commotion,
    At the bidding of thy will.

" Thus my heart the hope will cherish,
    While to thee I lift mine eye ;
Thou wilt save me ere I perish,
    Thou wilt hear the sailor's cry.
And though mast and sail be riven,
    Life's brief voyage will soon be o'er,
Safely moor'd in heaven's wide haven,
    Storm and tempest vex no more."

MADNESS FROM STRONG DRINK.

Mr. Scroesby, chaplain of the Liverpool (Eng
land) Mariner's Church, has written " An address

to Seamen, on Improvidence and Intemperance.
The following are extracts from it

"As to lunacy or madness, it is an important
and awful fact, that the great majority of cases of
this distressing disease, are clearly ascertained to
be the consequence of drunkenness. A distinguished friend of my own, in the medical profession, who has had extensive experience in respect
to this malady, declares, that more than one-half,
and probably three-fourths of the cases of lunacy
which have come under his notice, were produced
by excessive drinking! And at a meeting of the
Middlesex magistrates, for considering the cause
and remedy of the dreadful evils of drunkenness,
it was stated, that about a year ago, there were 825
wretched inmates in the 'Pauper Lunatic Asylum,' but they had of late increased to 1,200,
which was mainly attributable to gin drinking!
A similar result, which too satisfactorily corrobo-
rates what has already been stated, is obtained
from the intelligent governor of the *Liverpool Lunatic Asylum.* In four years, 495 patients were
admitted into the Asylum, of which number, it has
been sufficiently ascertained, that there were 257
at least, who had brought on their derangement by
excessive drinking."

WHO SLEW THESE?

"ONE man, when in a state of intoxication, fell
into the 'hot-water tub' of a brewer, and was
scalded to death; and several different persons
fell into the docks or river, whilst drunk, and were

drowned. A female, having been drinking in a
public house, received an injury in a quarrel, of
which she almost immediately died; another woman, much addicted to drinking, was burnt to
death; another of similar habits, when 'apparently tipsy,' jumped out of a window and was
killed! One man met with death by drinking in
a very extraordinary manner. Leaning on the
side of a puncheon of rum lying on the side of one
of the docks, he indulged himself in the stolen
draught, by sucking it through a reed, the effect
of which was almost immediately fatal. Another
man, who had been very much intoxicated the
night before, under the depression of returning
sobriety, cut his throat; and another of similar
habits hanged himself! One person, in a more
respectable situation of life, ' died of a disease of
the lungs, hurried on by excessive drinking.' Two
boatmen, in a drunken quarrel on the river, fell
overboard, and 'were drowned. One individual,
when half intoxicated, fell only from the steps in
front of a house, and was killed on the spot. Another unhappy man, who had just been released
out of jail, went almost direct to a public house,
and drank four glasses of rum; from thence he
went home and took some supper, but with a thirst
irresistibly excited by his previous drinking, he
proceeded again to the scene of his self-indulgence,
and such was the effect, that on his return to his
residence he fell into a lethargic sleep, from which
he never awoke! A woman accustomed to drinking, accompanied a sister in iniquity to a social
revel, where they drank till intoxicated : then,
returning to the house which one of them occupied, they went together to bed, but, during the
night, one was taken to an eternal world, whilst

the other slept! Another wretched creature, pursuing the same destructive habit, was returning to her house in a state of drunkenness, 'when she fell into the opening of a cellar and was killed on the spot!

INTEMPERANCE AMONG SEAMEN.

"AND the great day of account will bear terrible witness, when the 'sea shall give up the dead that are in it,' of the vast and unsuspected extent of the sacrifice of life among seamen, from shipwrecks and other catastrophies, occasioned by drunkenness. One distressful instance, among the numbers that will hereafter be brought to light, occurred within my own observation. A collier brig was stranded on the Yorkshire coast, and I had occasion to assist in the interesting but distressing service of rescuing a part of the crew, by drawing them up a vertical cliff two or three hundred feet in altitude, by means of a deep-sea lead line, the only rope that could be procured. The first two men who caught hold of this slender line were hauled safely up the frightful cliff; but the next, after being drawn to a considerable height, slipped his hold, and he fell; and with the fourth and last, who ventured upon this only chance of life, the rope gave way, and he also was plunged into the foaming breakers beneath! Immediately afterwards the vessel broke up, and the remnant of the ill-fated crew, with the exception of two, who were washed into a cavern in the cliff, perished before our eyes! But what was the cause

of this heart-rending event? Was it stress of
weather, or bewildering fog, or unavoidable accident? No! it arose entirely from the want of
sobriety; every sailor, to a man, being in a state
of intoxication. The vessel, but a few hours before,
had sailed from Sunderland; the men being drunk,
a boy, unacquainted with the coast, was intrusted
with the helm: he ran the brig upon Whitby
Rock, and one-half of the miserable, dissipated
crew awoke to consciousness in eternity! To this
solitary instance, I might add many more; but
this must suffice, both as to illustration and proof
of the terrible consequences of intemperance at
sea."—*Scoresby's Address.*

NAVY.

WE hear it frequently said, and sometimes when
it ought not to be said, that seamen are desperately depraved and dissipated, ignorant, bigoted, and
hardened in vice: that the necessary police and
discipline of a ship of war, is adapted to humble
them to meanness; to destroy every vestige of
self-respect and manly dignity; and consequently,
to depress ambition, and confirm these deplorable
habits and propensities. And it is pertinently
asked, "Under such circumstances what can reclaim
them?" We answer: A sovereign remedy for all
this, opposing difficulties and deeply-rooted moral
diseases, is an enlightened and regular ministration
of the Gospel of Christ. He is the physician who
has prescribed this specific, and will administer it
to their cure if it be furnished. This will enlighten.

reform, and liberalize officers and men. Let there
be no alcohol in any of its forms, but in the doc
tor's medical stores: let flogging be suppressed,
and other modes of punishment substituted, and
regulated by courts-martial, according to crime;
give them the Bible, the Seamen's Magazine, and
suitable tracts; and back all, by sending on board
of every ship of the line, every frigate, and every
sloop of war, an enlightened, discreet, evangelical,
and efficient chaplain. Let the schoolmaster, in all
cases, be a man of practical godliness; and then
let the cabin and the ward-room countenance and
encourage the herald of the cross, and you have
the grand catholicon, which will soon change every
ship's company into as moral, Christian, and orderly a community, as any of our country societies
generally are: and under the light and power of
divine truth, you will find convictions and conver-
sions as frequent in the navy, in proportion to their
numbers, as you will ordinarily in all our congre-
gations on shore: and all this you will see is practicable, and of easy accomplishment.—*Mr. E.
M'Laughlin's Letter to the Secretary of the A. T.
Society.*

THE CARTER OF DUNDEE.

To Seamen.

BROTHER sailors: having passed a good part of
my life among you, I really feel more regard for
you than for any other of my countrymen. My
early recollections, my most endearing associations
are connected with your profession; and I shall

never in this life covet a higher or more honorable
title, than that of an honest British tar. The
character of the British sailor is esteemed all over
the world. Shall we not all, as individuals, do
what we can to render ourselves worthy of such a
profession? To encourage ourselves in some mea
sure to do so, is the aim of the following remarks.

You are aware that spirit-drinking is very prevalent among us. Nothing can be more pernicious
and more opposed to our real interest; leading as
it does, directly to poverty, ignorance, infamy, disease and death. In consequence of the habit acquired by many of us, of seeking gratification in
the use of intoxicating liquors, we are kept in con-
tinual poverty, not only by the expense incurred
in perpetually supplying this gratification, but by
the means of various snares and temptations to
which drinking exposes us, particularly in the
company of sharpers, pickpockets, and impostors;
for you well know, how easily seamen in a state of
intoxication are robbed, cheated, and flattered out
of their well-earned and far-sought wages. I would
beseech you, therefore, to think of the dangers to
which you are exposed; to the hunger, thirst, cold,
and hardships you endure in obtaining your money;
and of the folly and stupid madness of squander-
ing it away on an article like ardent spirits, which
is not only useless, but pernicious.

Perhaps some of us imagine, that ardent spirits
add to the strength of our bodies. This is a mis
take. There is nothing in them according to the
most eminent doctors, of a nourishing property, unless it be the portion of water which they contain
they stimulate, and produce an excitement for a
short time; but this is invariably followed by a
greater or less degree of lassitude, langor and fa.

tigue; so that so far from strengthening the body, they absolutely render it weaker, and at last cause disease and premature old age. But I may here appeal to the personal experience of many of my brother sailors. Do you not enfeeble your bodies more in the course of a few weeks on shore, while you are spending your money, than you did in the months or years during which you were earning it? Now, keeping out of sight the contagious diseases you are exposed to from your vicious companions; the dangerous colds brought on by exposure after intoxication; the many wounds, bruises, and injuries you meet with by falls, fighting, or otherwise: I say, even keeping all these out of sight, the mere habitual use of spirits brings on a great variety of diseases, and very often leads to sudden death, because they give a strong excitement without nourishment, and drive on the human system at a quicker rate than its all-wise Maker intended. The man who seeks strength by the use of ardent spirits, acts like a ship-master, who, when his ship is tender and in danger of upsetting, sets more sail, in order to relieve her. And what should we think of the man, who would keep us constantly employed in setting up our rigging, adding tackle to tackle, and purchase upon purchase, and wringing it down without relaxation or intermission? We know very well, that however strong it might be at first, it would in the end tumble about our ears. The same foolish conduct with respect to our bodies, must produce the most disastrous consequences. But suppose, that after we have carried a press of sail for a length of time, our rigging becomes slack, and that after having been long at sea, and laboring hard, the seams of our vessel have loosenod and widened, and that she has in conse-.

quence become leaky, would we carry more sail to
lighten our rigging, or would we take our vessel
into a heavier sea to close her seams and stop her
leaks? Yet this is the way many of us take with
our bodies; when we are overstrained with labor,
we drink ardent spirits, which excite us still more,
and even sleep in such circumstances yields no re-
freshment. Is it not, therefore, the height of
madness, to use an expensive and hurtful excitement, for which, in a state of health, there is no
manner of necessity? We are, in fact, capable of
undergoing all ordinary fatigue and labor with the
strength conferred upon us by our Creator, and
have no need of artificial force.

There are a number of Christians among seamen,
and let me direct the attention of such individu
als to the awful consequences of intemperance on
those around them. When they see its ravages
even in this life, did the evil go no farther, they
would find enough to awaken the kindest sympathies, to arouse the strongest energies of their nature, to call forth their Christian love: and when
they see the people among whom their lot is cast,
heedlessly rushing on to, and madly and eagerly
preparing themselves for everlasting destruction,
how great, how powerful is the appeal! They will
try all means; and let them among other means
form Temperance Societies. Let them do so in
the name of our Lord Jesus Christ, who although
he was rich, yet for our sakes became poor, that
we through his poverty might become rich. Let
them become instruments in the hand of God, to
arrest the pestilence which, like a blasting mildew,
has overspread the land, and will continue to weak-
en the strength, and corrupt the morals of our beloved country. Unless the temperate unite in a

stern and unyielding abstinence from this body-
and-soul-destroying agent, it will continue to ruin
our physical, moral, and intellectual energies, and
weaken the wooden-walls of old England, more
than the dry-rot of her timbers, or the most powerful foreign enemy. Now, my dear friends and fel-
low-seamen, if you have a regard for your own
interest; if you have any respect to character; if
you have any attachment to those around you; if
you are lovers of your country; if you love your
children; and above all, if you love your God, I
beseech you rally round the standard of temperance, and by God's blessing, we shall be the means
of working to his glory and to our country's
good.—*Wm. Cruickshank.*

ODE TO RUM.

" HAIL! mighty Rum! the drunkard's greatest joy
And let thy praise my willing pen employ:
From east to west thy mighty deeds are known,
From humble peasant to the royal throne.
Where'er thou dost thy mighty sceptre sway,
Obsequious homage all thy subjects pay;
To thee devote their bodies and their souls,
And sing thy praise around their flowing bowls.
At thy command both sense and reason fly,
Riches and honor pine away and die:
Domestic peace thou hast the power to kill,
Where thou dost fix thine empire in the wil..
Both kings and mighty warriors thou hast slain;
Made prostrate heroes press the sanguine plain:
Their thousands slain, the sons of Mars may boast,
But thou hast tens of thousands in thy toast.
Inspired by thee thy votaries dare to face
Pale poverty, disease, and foul disgrace;
While in thy service they are not dismayed,
At death and hell in awful forms portrayed.

Thy magic power can clamorous conscience still,
And banish all the fears of future ill;
And those who serve thee faithful to the end,
Need never hope to find a better friend."
Sailor's Magazine.   ANTI BACCHUS.

HOW THE SABBATH MAY BE SANCTIFIED AT SEA.

"REMEMBER the Sabbath-day to keep it holy.'
The Sabbath is to be remembered, not only as a
day of bodily rest, that it be not profaned; but as
a day of spiritual activity, that it be sanctified. It
is not enough that we refrain from worldly labor,
for our ox and our ass may do that, but we must
engage in heavenly duties. For, at the same time
it is our duty to deny ourselves the search after
worldly pleasure or worldly profit; it is equally
our duty to seek for spiritual enjoyments and the
profit of the soul. And whilst we are called upon
to distinguish the Sabbath-day from all other days,
we are likewise positively charged, if we would
have a blessing from God thereon, to "call the
Sabbath a delight, the holy of the Lord, honorable."

Let us, then, consider how we may so hallow
the Sabbath, that we may glorify God, and derive
spiritual blessings for ourselves. These two things,
indeed, always go together. If we earnestly seek
the glory of God, we certainly shall receive blessings on our own souls. This being the case, we
shall principally confine our remarks to the means
of sanctifying the Sabbath at sea, in order to spiritual edification.

Though there be no " sound of the church-going

bell," to call you to the duty of public prayer;
though you have no sacred temple in which to present yourselves unto the Lord ; and no consecrated
priest to minister in holy things ; yet it is as much
your duty to remember the Sabbath at sea, and to
endeavor to sanctify it, as it is to keep it holy on
shore. And I must be free to tell you, th: t if yo
excuse yourselves, the Lord excuseth you .ot. I
makes no exception for sailors. Does an, one say,
that it is not possible to serve the Lord at sea?
We cannot keep the Lord's day holy? We cannot
have divine service on each returning Sabbath?
Mistaken friends, allow me to say *you can*. The
word of God says *you must*. If you cannot serve
God at sea, you ought to stay on shore. If your
profession prevents you from being good Christians,
holy men, let me tell you, it is a bad profession!
But I thank God it is otherwise. Neither your
occupation as sailors, nor the want of churches to
which you may resort, necessarily prevents you
from leading a holy and religious life. For the
Lord, who restricts not his servants to approach
him only in houses made with hands, can be wor-
shipped where no such churches exist, afar off at
sea, even as on shore. Because, " wheresoever two
or three are gathered together in the name of
Christ," there hath he promised to be in the midst;
there is a church, and you may seek and expect a
blessing. And as to opportunity, there is abundance if you would improve it : if you have the will,
you will find the way. Gales, or dangers, or difficulties, though they occur in their usual course,
will seldom prevent your waiting on God, if you
be in earnest about this important duty. And this
fact I can speak to with confidence, because I have
proved it.

9*

In a voyage (the Greenland whale fishery,) much more perplexing, and much more subject to sudden embarrassments and dangers than the voyages commonly pursued, I have known public worship to be carried on so regularly, that never a Sabbath passed over, for several years together, without one or more full services being performed. In almost every case, indeed, during the time referred to, there were two regular services, after the form of the Church of England, including the singing of psalms and the reading of a sermon, besides short prayers, and the catechizing of the apprentices in the evening. During these voyages, severe gales have commenced on the Sunday; dangers from rocks, ice, and lee-shores have threatened; frequent embarrassments from thick weather have occurred; yet time and opportunity were always found for the worship of God. The success of the voyage often seemed to be in the way; duty to the owners of the ship seemed to forbid; yet we persevered in waiting upon God, and certain I am we often found his blessing. In a few instances, indeed, the usual hour of worship could not be exactly kept; but an opportunity has always been found, of having each of the two services in succession, and generally the third, according to the plan I am about to suggest:

This plan, which, on account of its practical efficiency, I can confidently recommend, I shall now state; and may He whose worship and honor it is designed to promote, incline the heart of every reader to receive it, so far as it is applicable to the voyage and circumstances under which he sails; and may the same comfort and blessing be derived from the adoption of it, which the writer himself and his little church, have often been permitted to experience.

At three bells, (9½ A. M.) every Sunday morning, the hands were "turned up," to prepare themselves for the forenoon service; then, according to the state of the weather, or the accommodation we had in the ship, the church was either "rigged" upon deck, or arrangements made for divine service below. At eleven, the service commenced, and generally concluded a few minutes after twelve. From the calling of "all hands" until this time, every man was on Sabbath-day duty; and although no one was made to join in the prayers against his will, yet he had only this option, to watch or pray. Those, therefore, that declined to worship along with us,—who indeed, were very few,—kept watch upon deck, and were under the direction of the officer in charge of the ship, for the performance of any necessary duty till the prayers were ended, and then the watch was considered to be again set. At half-past three, (P. M.) the watch was called, and ten minutes afterwards, afternoon prayers commenced, and none of the people belonging to either of the watches were expected to retire below until the service was ended. By this arrangement the morning service was concluded at dinner time, and the hour for the afternoon service was taken equally out of the time belonging to the watches below. Again, at half-past seven, the apprentices, whom I considered almost as a filial charge, were called below, and after reading by alternate verses, two or three chapters out of the New Testament, were catechized concerning the same. And then, this evening service was concluded by singing and a short prayer. This service, however, was not confined to the apprentices; any of the sailors who liked to join us came down at the striking of seven bells, and some of them generally took their turn along with the apprentices in the reading of the Scriptures.

Before each of our services, whenever the wea·ther was at all unsettled, the ship was put under somewhat snug sail, and the deck being left to the charge of the proper officer of the watch, with the assistance of the helmsman, all the rest of the crew, or nearly all, could generally be spared to join in the public prayers. When, indeed, there was any probability·of squalls, or of any change being requisite in the sails, some few of the proper watch were placed within observation of the proper officer on deck, so as to be easily called up without disturbing their comrades ; but if circumstances had required, though for several years no such case ever occurred, the officer had orders to call up all the hands to assist him ; for the safety of the ship, or the security of her masts and sails, is such a necessity, as will well justify this temporary inter-ruption.

Such, my seafaring friends, is a sketch of the plan which I found particularly useful and practicable in carrying on Sabbath-day duties at sea. I ....ose particulars to you, by way of hints for your assistance, leaving them subject to such modifications as time and circumstances may require; yet feeling fully assured that you will find it of great advantage to begin upon some plan, otherwise unnecessary difficulties may arise, so as to discourage you from persevering in that duty, which from a strong conviction of its vast impor·tance,·I am most anxious to commend to you.

Such of you, my brethren, as approve of what has been advanced, will bear with me, while I offer

a few friendly suggestions by the way of further-
ing the important object of sanctifying the Sabbath. To this end, you will find it good to remember it before it arrives. Prepare for the day of
rest, as far as you can, on the Saturday. Let your
men have time, on Saturday evening, for those
needful acts of personal cleanliness which are better performed then than in the morning, so that
the Lord's day be not unnecessarily broken in upon
by these preparations. In every nautical duty
which requires attention on Sunday morning, bear
in mind the hours fixed for divine worship, that
every work that can possibly be anticipated may
be completed. If your flying sails be taken in,
your retirement will be the more comfortable and
secure, and you will seldom or never find the loss
in your voyage. "The Lord's blessing will abun-
dantly recompense this and every other sacrifice
made for his sake." Then call your men together,
as far as possible, at the appointed hour, either in
the cabin, or on the deck, as they may be most comfortable or convenient. Let the morning prayer
then be read with solemnity and devotion; the
chief mate, or any other person who is seriously
disposed, acting as clerk; and after the prayers it
will be proper and useful to read a sermon.

Again, in the afternoon, let your crew and passengers, if any, have the opportunity of "worship-
ping the Most High God, who made the heavens
and the earth, and the wide sea." And, whether
it be convenient to have any other service for the
benefit of your apprentices or not, you will find it
a good thing thus to wait upon the Lord: you will
experience a benefit temporally as well as spiritu-
ally; your people will be more orderly and respect-
ful; and Almighty God will be thy defence; for

then thou shalt delight thyself in the " Almighty
and shalt lift up thy face unto God; thou shalt
make thy prayer unto him, and he shall hear
thee "—*Rev. W. Scoresby.*

RELIGION IN SHIPS.

**THE DUTY OF CAPTAINS TO ENDEAVOR TO PROMOTE RE-
LIGION IN THE SHIPS UNDER THEIR COMMAND.**

BELIEVING captains! the spiritual interest of
your sailors is your special and responsible duty.
Was Eli, and the house of Eli judged forever for
the iniquity which Eli knew, when his sons made
themselves vile, and he restrained them not? Was
Abraham specially blessed, because he commanded
his household after him, that they should keep the
way of the Lord, and should do justice and judgment? Avoid ye, then, the curse of Eli, by neither
neglecting to care for the souls of your sailors, nor
refusing to restrain them so far as in you lies, in
unhallowed courses; seek ye the blessing of Abra
ham, by commanding your people to keep the day
of the Lord; to honor his Sabbaths; to reverence
his holy name; to fear an oath; and to exhibit
that correct and holy example, which may manifest
to the remotest regions of the earth, that ye are a
godly people. It is not in you, indeed, nor in the
power of any man, to make a wicked crew a religious people, for such a work is divine, and requires
the power of the living God; but it is in your
power to employ those means, and to enforce that
example which, though by possibility they may
fail to convert your crew, will not fail to return in

blessings upon your own souls. For be assured, that he that laboreth for the honor of Christ, shall not lose his reward. You shall have comfort among your people ; you shall have peace in your own bosoms ; you will win a blessing upon your voyage; your owners and merchants will be blessed in you ; and your present and eternal happiness will be greatly promoted. Thus shall you be advancing your temporal good, however transient, and laying up for yourselves treasures in heaven, where neither moth nor rust doth corrupt, nor any of the changes or misfortunes of this mortal life san injure or destroy.—*Rev. W. Scoresby.*

LOOK ALOFT.

" In the tempest of life, when the wave and the gale
Are around and above, if thy footing should fail,
If thine eye should grow dim, and thy caution depart,
' Look aloft,' and be firm and fearless of heart.

" Should they who are dearest, the son of thy heart,
The wife of thy bosom, in sorrow depart,
' Look aloft,' from the darkness and dust of the tomb,
To that soil where affection is ever in bloom.

" If the friend who embraced in prosperity's glow,
With a smile for each joy, or a tear for each woe,
Should betray thee when sorrows like clouds are arrayed,
' Look aloft' to the friendship which never shall fade.

" Should the visions which hope spreads in light to thine eye,
Like the tints of the rainbow, but brighten to fly,
Then turn, and through tears of repentant regret,
' Look aloft' to the sun that is never to set.

And oh ! when death comes in terrors to cast
His fears on the future. his pall on the past,
In that moment of darkness, with hope in thine heart,
and a smile in thine eye, ' Look aloft,' and depart."
                                        Sailor's Magazine.

THE ETERNAL SABBATH.

" Thine earthly Sabbaths, Lord, we love;
But there's a nobler rest above;
To that our longing souls aspire,
With ardent pangs of strong desire.

" No more fatigue, no more distress,
No sin nor hell shall reach the place;
No groans to mingle with the songs
Which warble from immortal tongues.

" No rude alarms of raging foes;
No cares to break the long repose;
No midnight shade, no clouded sun.
Obscures the lustre of thy throne

" Around thy throne, grant we may meet,
And give us but the lowest seat;
We'll shout thy praise, and join the song
Of the triumphant, holy throng.

FOR MY BIBLE.

" Almighty Father, Lord o'er all,
In mercy hear my feeble call;
And now thy Spirit give;
And while I read thy sacred page,
Still may thy word my grief assuage
And teach me how to live.

" O may it be my guide while here,
And quickly quell each raging fear,
While on thy name I cry;
And when my fleeting hours are past,
Then grant, O grant, it may at last
Support me when I die.

VOYAGE OF LIFE.

" When first we spread our tiny sails,
On life's eventful sea—
And gently wafted by the gales,
How full of life we be!

" Fierce, angry billows never rise,
    And all is smooth before,
And bright above, as if the skies
    Ne'er threatened aspect wore.

" Calm and serene, we banish fear,
    Nor dream of future ill;
No voice of danger cometh near,
    And all is joyful still.

" Thus onward by the gentle breeze,
    Our fragile bark is driven—....
Till in the wild and boisterous seas,
    We're tempest-tost and riven.

" When all is lost we look behind—
    For help we loudly cry;
We're answered only by the wind
    As it comes sweeping by.

" How blest is he in early youth,
    Who taketh for his chart,
That word which is eternal truth,
    And seals it in his heart.

" Though tempests beat upon his bark,
    And angry billows frown—
And all around is drear and dark—
    Success his efforts crown.

" Beyond the storm a light appears,
    The beacon light of faith;
It cheers his heart, and calms his fears,
    And takes the sting from death.

" Thus through his voyage propitious gales,
    With gentle seas are given—
Until at last he furls his sails,
    Safe in the port of Heaven.

                               D. C.

CONVERSION OF REV. JOSEPH EASTBURN.

Mr. Eastburn was the first stated preacher to seamen in Philadelphia, and, in fact, the first in the United States. He was born in Philadelphia, August 11, 1748. His parents were originally Friends, but being converted to experimental religion under the preaching of Mr. Whitfield, they left the Society of Friends, and united with other of Whitfield's converts, under the ministry of the Rev. Gilbert Tennent. Young Joseph was religiously educated, and his parents hoped he would eventually be a preacher; but his father, being taken prisoner by the Indians, rendered his parents too poor to give him any thing more than a common English education. At the age of fourteen, he was put apprentice to the cabinet-making business, in a large shop of seventeen thoughtless apprentices and young men. Here he was drawn away to break the Sabbath, by skating and other amusements, but soon his conscience was awakened, and he left his giddy companions, from whom he afterwards suffered much cruel mockery and persecution. What a strange exhibition of the human heart it is, that young men should so often take cruel delight in grieving one of their number, who is sincerely desirous of attending to religion, and saving his soul. But Joseph was unmoved by them, for he found these words continually coming to his mind, which he heard in a sermon by President Davies,—" Oh eternity! eternity! how will this awful sound echo through the vaults of hell!" For a long time he was in distress about his soul, and struggled to get sin out of his heart, while his wicked unbelief prevented him from coming to the

only Saviour, who can take away sin In an ao-
count of his early life, he says :—

"My mind was overpowered with unbelief, until
one Sabbath morning, about the break of day. I
was then thinking about my miserable state of
soul,—guilty, filthy, wretched, and helpless; and
that a Saviour was appointed, and Jesus was inviting me to come to him, and if I did, I should obtain relief. I found the hindrance was in myself,
and that none but the Lord could remove it. I
then fell on my knees, crying to him to undertake
for me. I tried to present all my wants to him,
and besought him, that whatever it was that hin-
dered my closing with Jesus, he would remove it
out of the way; and that he would be pleased to
work true faith in me, that I might believe. And
while I was thus pouring out my heart to the Lord
for his grace, that blessed counsel of the precious
Saviour was powerfully impressed on my mind,
contained in the third chapter of the Revelations,
18th verse,—' I counsel thee to buy of me gold
tried in the fire, that thou mayest be rich; and
white raiment, that thou mayest be clothed, and
that the shame of thy nakedness do not appear;
and anoint thine eyes with eye-salve that thou
mayest see." Now a perfect suitableness appeared
in this blessed provision to answer all my wants;
for I knew I was truly poor, and deep in debt to
divine justice, and had nothing of my own to pay.
But the white raiment was what I stood in particular need of, for I had often been filled with horror at the thought of appearing a guilty, vile, filthy
spirit, before the bar of a just and holy God; but
if arrayed in this glorious white raiment, I might
appear there to divine acceptance, and all my filthy
garments be cast away. The enlightening of the

mind with this eye-salve of the Holy Spirit, was
what I was likewise deeply sensible I greatly
needed; so that before I was aware of a change in
my mind, my soul cried out,—O Lord! I accept
this gracious counsel, and do bless thee for it. My
heart was filled with comfort, and I could now call
the Lord my dear Father, and felt my very soul
going out to him in love, whom before I had so
much dreaded as my awful Judge. I know not
that any creature heard me, in all or any of my
private exercises, or how long I continued in this;
but when I came down to my father's family, with
whom I then boarded, my father saw such a change
in my countenance, that he directly desired me to
lead in family worship, which I felt a willingness
to do."

HIS PREACHING TO THE SAILORS.

It appears by Mr. Eastburn's Journal, that
he began to preach statedly to seamen on the fourth
Sabbath in October, 1819. He says in his Journal for that day,—" Many attended, morning and
afternoon, and conducted very well. Some were
affected. On the third Sabbath of October of this
year, the present commodious Marine Church, in
Philadelphia, was opened for worship. A particular narrative of the efforts that had been made for
the accommodation of mariners with a place of
worship in that city, was at the time presented.
Some of the pious reflections contained in that narrative are worthy of being preserved.

    " The reflections arising from a review of the
peculiar smiles of Providence attending the efforts
using in favor of mariners, are calculated to fill the
mind with wonder and astonishment at the good

ness and mercy cf the Lord. Surely it conveys the encouraging hope, that the set time to favor seamen is come. The interest excited in their behalf, was simultaneous on both sides of the Atlantic. Only seven or eight years have elapsed since the public feeling has in any measure been alive to this object; and what has been the result, both in Europe and America, since that period? *Bethel Unions, Floating Chapels, Mariner's Churches, and Prayer Meeting Establishments,* we hear of, from almost every large seaport. Can this be any other than a supernatural influence operating at one and the same time, without concert, without the knowledge of each other's exertions; and yet, all tending to the same GODLIKE work of benevolence, the salvation of the souls of poor neglected mariners?

HIS DEATH.

" From the time this holy man began to preach to watermen, he devoted himself very much to their interests, and had the happiness to succeed in a remarkable degree in gaining their respect and confidence. What sailor that ever met Father Eastburn, did not love the old man? He preached to them, he visited them, he went on board their ships, and to their lodgings; he prayed with the sick; he attended the funerals of the deceased; he bore them on his heart to God in his private prayers; and in every way he sought to win their souls for Christ. And there is reason to believe he was successful in very many instances.

" From June, 1827, to the time of his death, he labored under an internal disease, beyond the reach of medicine. He never after attended the Mariner's Church but once.

10*

"In the month of September, he was once carried to his beloved Mariner's Church, where he
made a short address to the Sabbath-school children, and one still shorter to the mariners themselves. This was his farewell interview with them,
and was so regarded by all the parties concerned.
It is almost needless to say, that tears in abundance were shed on the occasion.

"After this he languished till the morning of
January 30, 1828, when he fell asleep in Jesus.
'Mark the perfect man, and behold the upright,
for the end of that man is peace.'

The name and virtues of Joseph Eastburn, (says
his biographer,) have probably been already celebrated in the four quarters of the globe. The last
ten years of his life were so disinterestedly, assid-
uously, and affectionately devoted to all the best
interests of seamen, that a large number of them
regarded him with the veneration and attachment
which dutiful children bear to a worthy parent;
and with their characteristic warmth of feeling,
there is little reason to doubt that they have proclaimed his praise in every region to which their
vocation has called them. Not only in many of
the seaports of our own continent, but on the coasts
of Asia and Africa, and in various ports of Europe,
we may believe that they have extolled his piety,
commended his benevolence, and exhibited him as
an example.

"And how, it may be asked, was this celebrity
and affectionate attachment obtained? Was it acquired by an illustrious parentage, by splendid
genius, by great talents, by distinguished erudition,
or by munificent donatives? Nothing, not an iota
of all this. The individual concerned was of humble birth, he had no pretensions to genius, no emi-

nence of intellectual powers or attainments, little learning, and but a scanty property. The whole must be attributed to simple, genuine, consistent, fervent, active, eminent piety. Of the influence and esteem which such a piety may secure to its possessor, by manifesting itself in all the forms in which it will, without seeking or expecting such an effect, become conspicuous, Mr. Eastburn was one of the most striking instances the world has ever seen."

FUNERAL OF A FAITHFUL MINISTER.

" FAR from affliction toil and care
　　The happy soul is fled ;
　The breathless clay shall slumber here,
　　Among the silent dead.

" The Gospel was his joy and song,
　　E'en to his latest breath ;
　The truth he had proclaim'd so long
　　Was his support in death.

" Now he resides where Jesus is,
　　Above this dusky sphere ;
　His soul was ripen'd for that bliss,
　　While yet he sojourn'd here.

" The sailor's loss we all deplore,
　　And shed the falling tear ;
　Since we shall see his face no more,
　　Till Jesus shall appear.

" But we are hast'ning to the tomb ;
　　Oh, may we ready stand ;
　Then, dearest Lord, receive us home,
　　To dwell at thy right hand."

Extract from a sermon preached by the Rev. Joseph Benson, on a funeral occasion:

"Instead, therefore, of grieving immoderately, that our friends have entered into rest before us, and gained the blessed port which we toil hard to find ; let us rather, out of love to them, rejoice at least that they are safe landed. And though we, their companions, are left behind, let us take comfort in considering it is but a little while. The time is fast approaching when we too shall make the land. While the prosperous gales of divine grace arising swell our sails, and waft our vessel towards the shore, the tide of some returning affliction will flow, and convey it into the heavenly harbor. Then our friends that went before, shall rejoice to see us arrive safe, and crowd to bid us welcome. And we, I doubt not, shall have the comfort of finding many escaped thither, under the direction of their invisible Captain and Pilot, concerning whom we had entertained a thousand distressing fears ; lest, during the storm and tempest, they had suffered shipwreck, and been lost amidst the raging billows. And oh ! what a meeting that shall be : what mutual joy and congratulations, increased and heightened by the great and threatening dangers the parties had passed through, and the narrow escapes they had had. Let us look forward to the happy time. Let us comfort our hearts with the prospect of it, amidst the winds and waves of this troublesome world.—*Sailor's Mag.*

THE HOPE OF HEAVEN OUR SUPPORT.

"When I can read my title clear
   To mansions in the skies,
I'll bid farewell to every fear,
   And wipe my weeping eyes.

Should earth against my soul engage,
    And hellish darts be hurl'd,
Then I can smile at Satan's rage
    And face a frowning world.

" Let cares, like a wild deluge come,
    And storms of sorrow fall;
May I but safely reach my home,
    My God, my heav'n, my all;

" There shall I bathe my weary soul
    In seas of heavenly rest;
And not a wave of trouble roll,
    Across my peaceful breast.

                WATTS.

THE LIFE-BUOY OF THE SOUL.

BY THE REV. C. S. STEWART, A.M , CHAPLAIN IN THE
U. S. NAVY.

" THE calling of the midnight watch first reminded two youthful voyagers on the distant Pacific, that the conversation in which they were engaged had been prolonged to an unreasonable hour. It was the signal for one, as an officer of the ship, to take the post of duty in command on deck; and the customary salutations of a separation for the night were abruptly and hastily interchanged. A careless spectator might not have observed any thing peculiar in the manner in which these were made, but one accustomed to the study of his fellows, would have read in the expressive grasp of a sailor's hand, and in the subdued tone of a manly voice, some unaccustomed state of mind, some deep feeling of the heart. Nor would he have been deceived in the fact, though he might have mistaken the cause.

" A cloudless, sultry, and listless day at the equator, had been suddenly succeeded by a gloomy and foreboding night, with every indication in a wild and ragged sky above, and a deeply-heaving and moaning sea below, of some further, and not distant change: a change which might come upon the lonely bark, with a power alike destructive, whether exhibited in the rending fury of the lightning, or in the desolation of a tornado. But it was not, that, under circumstances such as these, he was called upon to assume the responsibility of the deck, that the tones of sadness were distinguished in the sailor's voice, or that the trepidation of an agitated mind is imparted to his hand. No! To him the sea had lost its terrors. From early boyhood till now, in the fullness of his youth, he had been familiar with its fitful changes—had been lulled to his soundest slumbers by its storms, and gazed upon the most fearful of its tempests only as,

> ' A babe lists to music,
> Wondering, but not affrighted,'

" It was a moral cause operating within, and not the intimidating aspect without, that had given rise to the feeling existing in his bosom.

" In the providence of God, the instructions of the day had been of the most solemn and impressive kind. An instance of mortality had occurred in the ship's company, similar in its characteristics and appalling result, to the tens of thousands which in various sections of the world, testify to the existence of a pestilence, that, with uncontrolled devastation, ' walketh in darkness, and wasteth at noonday.' One of the most athletic and youthful of the crew; one, who but the day previous, had trod the decks as vigorous and elastic, and with a heart as thoughtless and as gay, as any of his companions; had, after the agony of a few hours, fallen into the arms of death; and with the dawn of the coming morning, was to be seen stretched on the forecastle, in the habiliments of the grave, awaiting, beneath the banner of his country, the hour when his body should be committed to the deep, there to rest ' till the sea shall give up the dead."

" So silently and so swiftly had the destroyer passed by, that many on board were ignorant of the visitation, till coming on deck, their eyes met the resistless evidence of it in the lifeless corpse of their fellow. The only expression that for a time was heard to re-echo from one and another, as the startling fact fastened itself upon them, was,—' Can it be possible that J—— is dead!' And for hours after, as if still incredulous of the reality, one and another might be seen slowly to approach his bier, and turning aside its star-spangled covering, by long and silent gaze on the fixed and death-like stricken features of the youthful victim, to assure themselves that the spirit had indeed forsaken its abode; while the half-suppressed sigh, and in some instances, the gathering tear, hastily brushed from a hardy cheek, told how reluctantly they yielded themselves to the unwelcome truth.

" It was after a day marked by scenes and impressions such as these, that the two individuals now introduced, had met each other on deck at the setting of the first night watch. Only one hour before their meeting, the body of their departed shipmate, with the solemn rites of a burial at sea, had been committed to a fathomless grave; and with every thought absorbed in the affecting event

which had befallen them, they involuntarily spoke
to each other of the frailty and uncertainty of life.
of the solemnity of death, and the eternity of bless-
edness and woe revealed to man in the word of
God.

"To the mariner these were unaccustomed
themes. But under the circumstances in which
they were presented, they commended themselves
to the strong emotions of his heart, with an awakening and subduing power. And so his companion
unfolded to him his own views of their importance
to the welfare of the immortal spirit, and at length,
urged upon him the necessity of an undelayed repentance towards God, and of faith in Jesus Christ.
His soul, under the conviction 'of sin, of righteousness, and of judgment to come,' melted into peni-
tence, and threw into his aspect and manner the
deep feeling of the moment at which the midnight
bell had summoned him to the duties of his office
in command of the succeeding watch. Happily,
the impressions thus received did not, as is often
the melancholy fact, prove transitory or inopera
tive, but resulted in a fixed state of mind, which
will be best understood from the language of the
individual himself in a conversation with his friend,
some few weeks after their occurrence.

"The ship having, in the intervening time, safely
doubled the 'Cape of Storms,' was now gallantly
ploughing her trackless way through the tropical
latitudes of the South Atlantic, with all her canvas
spread to the freshness of her favoring trade-winds.
Above the constellation of the Cross,

'Mid stars unnumbered,
And exceeding beautiful,'

shone brightly and conspicuously, the object of

untiring admiration and of heavenly thought, while a full-orbed moon cast her mild and silvery beams mildly over the surrounding waters below. The loveliness of the scene thus exhibited, had detained the friends till a late hour on deck, and the rapid approaches they were making to a port, at which a separation was expected to take place, led them to a review, in their conversation, of the period passed since the death of their shipmate.

"Conscious that a change, affecting his entire feelings and character, in relation to the welfare and destiny of the soul, had occurred within it, the young sailor had ventured to believe, that, 'through the washing of regeneration, and renewing of the Holy Ghost,' he was a new creature in Christ Jesus; and yielding himself to that peace of conscience and joy of heart, which such a persuasion alone can impart to a contrite spirit; he thus gave utterance and illustration to the affections of his bosom, while every feature of his countenance, moulded in manliness of beauty seldom surpassed, was filled with beamings the most ingenuous and attractive:

"'Oh! how different does life now appear to me, and how different death!—I recollect once to have been in circumstances in which I thought death inevitable. It was on board a small vessel, on the American coast, overtaken by a terrific gale, just at right-fall, in the vicinity of a dangerous and iron-bound island. Such was the violence of the tempest, that it soon became impracticable to carry the least canvas to keep the vessel off the shore, which, though not in sight, was known to be near; and it was less a surprising than a horror-thrilling sound, to hear the cry of 'breakers on the lee-bow!' made from the fore-deck before midnight; while the thunderings of a heavy surf came booming on

11

the ear, above the roar of the winds and the raging
of the sea. Every one believed an escape impos
sible; and as an only refuge, I seized a spar near
me, with the intention of lashing myself to it, when
the fearful concussion between the ship and the
rocks should be felt. Soon a long line of white
foam was distinctly seen through the darkness of
the night, swelling mast high, and then bursting
with tremendous force over the pointed summits of
a range of cliffs,—all was given up as lost! At
this instant, as if by miracle, our little bark was
swept past the danger, on the heavings of the very
billow which seemingly a moment later would have
hurled her to utter ruin; and we found ourselves
in comparative safety under the lee of the head-
land, which had so nearly proved fatal.

"'I have thought of the scene a hundred times
within the last few weeks, and of the vain refuge
to which I then looked for security and comfort.
Oh how different would my thoughts and feelings
now be, if placed in similar circumstances! Should
shipwreck and death now befall me, thanks be to
the grace of God, my dependence and consolation
would not be on a piece of timber, as perishable in
the war of elements, as my own strength would be
unavailing against their power; but,' elevating his
eyes to the heavens, and fixing them, filled with
confidence and joy on the emblem of the cross—
'IN THE HOPE OF SALVATION,'—'THE LIFE-BUOY
OF THE SOUL!'"—*Christian Keepsake.*

PITY THE POOR SEAMAN.

"O THINK on the mariner toss'd on the billow!
    Afar from the home of his childhood and youth;—
No mother to watch o'er his sleep-broken pillow,
    No father to counsel, no sister to soothe.

Alone, 'mid the wastes of the desolate ocean,
　His prison-house floats at the sport of the wind;
Leaving all that his bosom regards with devotion,
　Society, kindred, and country behind.

" Ah! little know ye, who are peacefully sleeping
　On home's downy pillow, unwaken'd and warm,
The woes of the seaman, his dreary watch keeping,
　Amid all the horrors of midnight and storm.

" Oh say! shall the man thus to banishment driven,
　From all that entwines round the bosom below,
Be sternly shut out from communion with heaven,
　And end his sad life in a mansion of woe?

" Pour, pour on his pathway of tempest and gloom,
　The radiant light of the Gospel of peace;
And Bethlehem's star shall his passage illume
　To the haven where darkness and tempest shall cease."
　　　　　　　　　　　　　　　　Sailor's Magazine.

INCIDENTS IN A SAILOR'S LIFE.

ADDRESSED TO SEAMEN.

Lafayette College, Easton, Dec. 6, 1842.

DEAR SIR,—Your Magazine for this month came
to hand last evening, and it immediately reminded
me of my promise to you while in New York. This
evening, while reading its pages, I saw a communication in relation to myself, which I knew at once,
to be the production of Captain P——. O, that I
had heeded his instructions, then given to me in
the spirit of prayer, as I believe they all were.
But those days are past, and cannot be recalled;
and although spent in rebellion, yet I trust, the
Lord will overrule all for good. I will now fulfil
my promise :—

Some months ago, while on my passage from the Island of Santa Cruz, in the West Indies, to Phil adelphia, I conceived the plan of making known to the world, and more particularly to my brethren of the sea, some of the workings of Divine Provi- dence on my sinful heart; and having heard that you were the seaman's friend, I resolved to write a short account of them to you, in the hope that they would meet your approbation, and that you would give them an insertion in the Sailor's Magazine. But on my arrival at Philadelphia, I showed them to a friend, who advised me to keep them until I would be able to correct them. This I intended to have done; but my time has been so closely occupied as to prevent me; and as you have re- quested a copy, I will leave this with you, if you will do me the favor to correct any grammatical errors which you may detect, as well as those in the notation. I send this forth to the scrutinizing eye of the world, with many prayers to the God of the sea, that this bread, cast as it is upon the bosom of the waters, may return after many days. The fol lowing statement is intended by the writer, to carry to the mind of the reckless wanderer of the deep

" That there is One above all others,
        Who well deserves the name of friend,
    Whose love is far beyond a brother's,
        Full and free, and knows no end."

One,
    " Who plants his footsteps on the sea,
        And rides upon the storm;"

who is continually watching over the interests of the sailor; whose sceptre is extended to all who will receive pardon at his hands. Yet I hope, should some landsman overhaul it, that he will perceive in it the wondrous workings of the Holy Spirit, and apply them also to himself; as my object is not to be known in the world, but to do good in the cause of my Redeemer.

My dear shipmates, if the experience of one who has been a wanderer on the great deep for ten years, both in men-of-war and merchantmen; who has witnessed the effects of the wild tornado, the typhoon and hurricane; the ravages of death in all the various forms which he assumes on the deep; who at one time has seen his shipmates crushed by falling from aloft; and at another time, watched the horrid and rapid progress of the cholera take away thirty of them in one week;—on another voyage, who witnessed the departure of eighteen by sickness and intoxication; and again beheld the mournful spectacle of five, swimming about the vessel, while the hurricane was pouring forth its maddening fury. and lashing the waves to anger, so that it was utterly impossible to save them; together with many other such scenes, which time and opportunity would fail me to relate:—if, having shared the same perils and dangers in storm and tempest,—at sea and on shore,—at midnight and noonday,—aloft and below: and added to these, was himself sunk in the depths of debauchery and licentiousness, from which he has been snatched by the hand of the Lord,—" as a brand from the burning:"—if, I repeat it, such a one can sympathize with you in your neglected state, and claim your attention, then may I proceed to give you a brief narrative of ten years' cruisings. I have been led to take this step from pure love to your souls; hoping that a word from one of your own class and profession, may have more influence over you than the advice of a landsman, who cannot know what

11*

we know, unless they follow us on our voyages, and endure with us the trials enumerated here.

You may think, perhaps, I am a long time getting under weigh; but hold on a little longer, and I think I will satisfy you. It has been said by many seamen, myself among the number, that it was a matter of impossibility to serve God on board a vessel at sea, especially when a greater part of the crew are irreligious But I can safely aver, that this is an erroneous impression, under which the unconverted sailor often labors. That it is a trial, I will allow, and a very great one; but where is the trial too great for the Lord to overcome, or the work too hard for him to perform? None! I say, and so will every one else say, who acknowledges his power. Did he not save Noah, when the whole earth was deluged with the flood? Did he not bring Joseph out of the hands of Potiphar, and set him over all the land of Egypt? Did he not save Moses in the ark, though the edict had gone forth from Pharaoh to destroy all the males of the Hebrews? Did he not save righteous Lot? Deliver Job? Save Jonah from the jaws of the sea-monster? Bring the children of Israel out of Egypt? divide the waters of the Red Sea for them, and sink their enemies in its waves? Did he not save Peter, when he cried, " Lord, save, or I perish?" Methinks you will say, Yes. Hence can he not, *will he not* save you from the revilings of a few blasphemous shipmates? He will! he will! He has delivered me, and set me in a way to honor him; and he will you also, if you cast your care upon him:—

' Venture on him; venture wholly !
Let no other care intrude."

I have told you, that he has snatched me " as a brand from the burning," and will now tell you how he has done it. I left my home at the early age of 13 years, in June 1831, although rather against my parents' will ; and all the scenes through which I have been called to pass since then, arose, in the providence of God, from so trivial a circumstance as that of breaking a pane of glass ; for, directly after the accident, I made the resolution to follow the sea ; and what renders it more singular, was the fact, that up to that hour, I had held every thought of the sea in perfect abhorrence.   My parents had taught me to obey them strictly, and had set before me examples of morality.   I soon made known to them my wishes and ideas in relation to a sea life, but they strenuously forbade me to think of it any more.

I did not openly rebel, or answer to their injunctions ; but they soon discovered by my actions that the desire to go to sea, was the leading object of my mind, and it appeared to them that nothing else could satisfy me.   Therefore, after many petitions on my part, and repeated denials on theirs, they at last conceded to my wishes, and I set out, young and inexperienced, to seek my fortune on the restless and fathomless waters of the great deep.   A FOREMAST HAND.

To be continued.

CHRIST STILLING THE TEMPEST.

' 'TWAS midnight,—and a lonely bark
    Was tossing on deep Galilee,
Without one star, to light the dark
    And angry billows of the sea.

Ar.d in that bark, a precious band
Of noble heart, and manly form,
Link'd soul with soul, and hand to hand,
Braved manfully the raging storm.

But wind and wave warr'd fierce and long,
Till hope seemed past, and ruin near,
And hearts that late were firm and strong,
Bowed down in agony and fear.
And broken cries, and fervent *prayer*,
Went up amid the angry blast,—
Woe, for the weary toilers there,
Had *this* lone refuge failed at last!

"But ah! what strange, majestic form,
Is that which cometh o'er the sea,
With footsteps firm, amid the storm,
Walking the wave so fearlessly?
Awe-struck—their spirits sink as dead,—
But soon again—they leap—rejoice—
As—'It is I! be not afraid,'
Breaks from the blessed MASTER's voice.

"Again He spake—'Peace—peace—be still!'
And trembling at His high behest,—
The angry surge obeyed His will,
And winds and waves were hush'd to rest
Oh! in that voice—what *love* and *power*,
To soothe the trembling—rule the wave,
Were manifested in that hour,
Of rescue from a watery grave.

"THOU, that didst rule wild Galilee
When hope's last star had dimly set,
O! calm the billows of *life's* sea,
For *it* hath weary voyagers yet.
Still every wave of passion's flow,
Rebuke each rising tide of sin,
And let each trusting spirit know,
The bliss of *perfect peace* within.'

Troy, Feb. 1847.   IDA.

INCIDENTS IN A SAILOR'S LIFE.

ADDRESSED TO SEAMEN. (*Continued.*)

Lafayette College, Jan. 1843.

My Dear Sir,—In my last, I told you that I
left a quiet home to seek my fortune on the ocean.
I need not tell you, however, that it was but a
ragged one: yet I could expect nothing better,
while leading a life of open rebellion against my
God. I left my dear mother on the morning of
the 6th of June,—'twas a Sabbath morning; I well
remember how she wept, and how little I felt the
separation at the time. I had been looking earnestly for the period of my departure to arrive,
that I might realize all the delights my delusive
imagination had conjured up in my mind. I felt
a small pang at parting with my mother, and brothers, and sisters, which increased as the time for
separation decreased; but in a few moments I
found myself walking at a smart pace towards the
river Thames, my father leading me by the hand.
About seven o'clock, we embarked on board the
steamboat " Thames," bound to Plymouth, where
lay the man-of-war, on whose books my name was
enrolled for a three years' cruise.

The vessel proceeded down the river at a rapid
rate until she arrived off North-Fleet, where she
lay to for a few minutes, to set some passengers
ashore, among whom was my father. He came to
me and kissed me: "Good bye, my son," said he;
and after pressing his quivering lip to my cheek,
he hurried into the boat. I had, on my way down
the river. been watching the sparkling waters as
they were thrown aside by the vessel's prow, and

fallen into somewhat of a revery, in which I thought only of the scenes of the future, and from which I was only awakened by the vessel again forging ahead. I then felt that I was alone in the world, and had but a faint recollection of the parting with my father. I felt as though the events which had passed, were but a shadow or a dream. However, the sparkling waves soon called off my attention again, and I was lost in delight as before. Sometimes I would look among those around for an answer to some question in relation to the passing objects, and then again turn to the heaving spray. I anxiously and vainly waited in expectation of seeing the waves rise to mountainous heights, as my young mind had pictured them while reading some tale of the sea, long before I had dared even to think of casting myself on the mercies of the relentless waves. Two days and nights passed on board the steamboat, and on Thursday morning I landed in Plymouth, and immediately took a boat and proceeded on board my floating home. I was a little strange at first, but soon became reconciled to my new companions,—who were, by the bye, not of the most virtuous stamp; yet, I found it necessary that I should become as one of them. To do this, it was also necessary to ape their manners, and follow them in their initiatory scenes of wickedness.

Three months of the time passed slowly away on board of the hulk, and on the 5th of September I left Plymouth Sound, on board His Majesty's sloop " Pylades," of 18 guns, on a voyage for three years, to the coast of South America. I was seasick for three days, but after that, enjoyed perfect health the whole voyage.

A few evenings after our departure from the

land, the hands were turned up to *da nce and sky-lark*, which continued while the weather would permit, the whole cruise; and in which I almost invariably engaged. On one of these occasions, my mind recurred to the Sabbath school, which I had left the Sabbath previous to my departure; and I stole away from my companions, and crept in amidships, on the grating beside the cook's funnel. There I began to weep, but not alone,—there was another in whose breast a kindred spirit glowed. He was a boy of my own age; he had also been warned by his Sabbath school teacher, to pray to the God of the great waters; and he had forgotten him, " who counts the sea as the drop of the bucket, and the isles as a very little thing," till now: he crept away in the darkness, and hid himself with me to weep over sin. We were, perhaps, the only two hearts on board the vessel, at that hour, that wept on account of sin. (for weep we did), while all around us the shrill fife and bellowing drum, sent forth their cheering sounds to enliven the hearts of the ship's crew. Very near to where we were sitting, some told their adventures; others under the lee of the long-boat, were spinning yarns, some of which, for veracity, could not be excelled by a Gulliver or a Munchaussen; and, for length, exceeded even the good ship's maintop-bow-lines themselves. Still we wept, and wept bitterly too; wishing from our hearts, that some of the men could hear our resolves, and punish us if we broke them. While we were thus ruminating, it struck eight bells, and in the next instant the boatswain piped " down all hammocks," which put an end to our colloquy. This ended the first, and, I think, the last deep and pungent conviction for sin, that we experienced on board that vessel.

Very shortly after that period I became hard
ened, and, before I was fourteen years of age, a
drunkard, from which time, I drank all that came
within my reach ; and full often have I assisted to
stow away the liquor smuggled on board, in the
captain's cloak-bag, by the cockswain of the gig.
But to enter into minute details of all that hap-
pened on board that vessel would be superfluous,
and only presuming on your time and patience.
Suffice it then to say, that if death could have
made an impression on my heart, I should not
have been so far on the road to ruin ;—for my
shipmates were more than once dashed to pieces almost by my side.   I saw, too, in that vessel, what
but few men see at sea, *dying on one side, flogging
on the other, and cutting throats amidships*, and receiving a blow myself, for attempting to prevent
one from completing the diabolical purpose of taking his own life.   However, after having cruised
around the coast of Brazil, Chili, and Peru, en-
countering some heavy gales on both sides of the
Horn, I returned to my home, no more the innocent boy I was when I left it, but a hardened
drunkard at the age of sixteen.

After a short stay of three months at home, I
again bade farewell to home and friends, and exchanged them all to resume my wandering on the
blue waste of waters.

In a few days after, having received on board
300 convicts, with whom we were to sail to New
South Wales, the cholera morbus broke out, and
took away some five and six in a night.   On this
voyage, however, I thought but little of the kind
Guardian of all my ways.   There were some sea-
sons in which the Sabbath school instruction would

flit across my mind, but they were only momen tary, and were driven from me by the foul fiend Satan; while he filled my mind with such objections as these:—"You will have abundance of time for these things when you are an old man— you are young yet. How do you suppose you will get along in this world, if you give way to these nonsensical ideas? Leave these for older heads than yours. What is the use of this life, if you do not enjoy its pleasures while here? Take your shipmates' motto for your own, "A short life, if it may be; but a merry one, at all risks.'" Thus he continued to deceive me, and I to believe him. I gave way with reckless stupidity to his liberal injections of wickedness, and by these means sunk deeper and deeper in my career of iniquity. I made three successive voyages to the East Indies, and New South Wales, in English merchant vessels, until November 1839. In the course of God's providence, the vessel to which I belonged ran into Port St. Louis, in the Mauritius, and after having discharged her cargo, was chartered to convey a cargo of silk and tea, belonging to an American vessel that had been abandoned there, to the United States. I arrived in this happy country in February, 1840; and immediately commenced a series of debaucheries, which eventually caused me to leave my vessel. Nor did I want for pretended friends, who persuaded me to leave her. There I first became acquainted with that class of men, whose rapacious ways I hate, but whose souls I love,—I mean the sailor's landlord, the grog-shop friend. that is, while his money lasts. At my own home, I had no intercourse with such men; it was not. though, because there were none in London,

but because I lived with my parents, and did not
come under their influence.

A FOREMAST HAND

To be continued.

---

* With much fair speech she caused the youth to yield;
And forced him with the flattering of her tongue.
I looked and saw him follow to her house,
As goes the ox to slaughter; as the fool
To the correction of the stocks ; or bird
That hastes into the subtle fowler's snare,
And knows not, simple thing, 'tis for its life.
I saw him enter in, and heard the door
Behind them shut; and in the dark still night,
When God's unsleeping eye alone can see,
He went to her adulterous bed. At morn
I looked, and saw him not among the youths.
I heard his father mourn, his mother weep :
For none returned that went with her.   The dead
Were in her house; her guests in depths of hell ;
She wove the winding-sheet of souls, and laid
Them in the urn of everlasting death."

Pollok's Course of Time

INCIDENTS IN A SAILOR'S LIFE.

ADDRESSED TO SEAMEN.   (*Continued.*)

Lafayette College, Feb. 1843.

DEAR SIR,—Subsequent to my arrival in New
York, I made one voyage to the southward, and
three to Europe ; during which time my moral
character became more and more degraded.   It
will be necessary, however, to make some remarks
here on the abounding goodness of God, during
this time, inasmuch as I grew worse as I grew

older, and he did not leave me to myself. I had left my ship, on my first voyage, in Savannah; there I sold my clothes, and spent my money before it was due, for the purpose of satisfying my appetite for drink, *so intolerable had it become.* I shipped again for Liverpool, left my vessel there, and joined the ship Harkaway, of New York. On the Saturday before we sailed, Captain P—— came forward, and affectionately invited us to go to church on the morrow, giving as a reason, that we were about to sail on the Tuesday, and that we ought to take the love of God with us. He spoke of the Saviour's calling the fishermen from the shores of Galilee, to be his disciples, and of his willingness to receive sailors now, and closed his interesting discourse by exhorting us all to become Christians. There may, perhaps, be some whose eyes will rest on this, and who will remember that short sermon delivered by Captain P——, some, who perhaps stood by with me, and heard those words of exhortation, and like me, slighted them; should this meet the eye of such a one, to him let me say, " Obey, and you'll be saved." For you must give an account of it at the bar of God.

" I went, on the next day, to the Seamen's Bethel, and there, for the first time, heard prayers offered up for the sailor, and for our own ship and crew, too. This was something strange to me, but I supposed it was a special favor granted to the captain by the minister, on account of a former friendship. I had not then any conception of the brotherly love which reigns in the heart of Christians. On the first Sabbath after our departure, the captain called the crew and passengers aft, and read to us the prayers of the Church of England, and also explained them to us. This he did every

Sabbath, when wind and weather would permit
If the weather would not admit of worship on
deck, he took us into the cabin, and spent about
one hour and a half in prayer, and explained the
Scriptures; which were generally the subject of
scorn and derision among the crew, in the forecastle.   A library was also brought on deck, and
distributed among those who were inclined to read.
I often murmured because the books were all religious, and could take no pleasure in reading them.
At the end of the voyage, I was called into the
cabin to receive my wages, and there the captain
(unwilling that my blood should be on his skirt)
again affectionately invited me to turn to the Lord;
he predicted my future conversion, but it appeared
very far off to me.   His discourse on that occasion
affected me so much that I must have wept, had
not one of my shipmates entered the cabin at the
time, which made me afraid of being ridiculed.   I
therefore immediately made my exit.   I did not
follow the advice of the captain.   There was on
board that vessel one on whose mind the captain's
instructions had made some deep impressions.   I
sought him out directly he came on shore, and I
found him at the Sailor's Home, but took very
good care that he did not remain in the house
long.   I led him into the company which I myself
kept, and under my tuition, he soon lost all serious impressions.   In my company the prayer-
meeting was set aside, and the preference given
to the theatre.   In a few days we separated; but
not till I left him as deep in the "gall of bitterness and in the bond of iniquity" as myself.   I
shipped in the brig Billow, bound to Rochelle, in
France, and continued in the same blasphemous
way of living, until the passage was half made.

then the Lord arrested me again, through the
instrumentality of a tract called the "Swearer's
Prayer." On the Sabbath morning one of my
shipmates handed some tracts to me, which he said
had been given him by a person in New York. I
read a few lines of one, and was immediately filled
with apprehensions for the safety of my soul, and
the souls of my shipmates. I knew not, previous
to that moment, that an oath was a prayer. A
thrilling sensation pervaded my whole frame. I
turned to my shipmates, and in a solemn manner
told them that, if that tract was true, we truly were
in a dangerous situation. They smiled, and turned
what I said into ridicule. I found that something
needed to be done, but I knew not what. I was
very anxious for the safety of my immortal soul.
I read my Bible, and occasionally reproved my
shipmates for swearing, which caused me still
more opposition. However, in my watch on deck,
near midnight, I felt that all would be lost unless
I prayed to God. But in my trouble I feared I
had been too wicked, and that God would not have
mercy on such a wretch as I was, and when I would
have prayed, I found within my bosom an enemy,
such as I had never dreamed of before. My own
heart opposed me, and I battled with it for a half
hour before I could fall on my knees. At length
the good spirit prevailed; I poured out my sup-
plications to God, in the name of Christ, as my
Sunday-school teachers had told me to do years before. I arose from my knees somewhat calmed in
my mind; but I went not again. The continued
scoffs of my shipmates had their effect upon my
partially subdued heart; for, after battling against
them for some two or three days, in my own
strength, it returned to its wonted hardness, and

all my resolutions to become temperate, which had
been made at this time, were abandoned. The
first evening after entering the port of Rochelle, I
went on shore with my shipmates, and despite of
all my promises to abstain, or the wrath of an an
gry God, which filled my mind with horror, and
caused me to tremble in every limb, I swallowed
the *intoxicating poison*, and then waited for death,
which I expected to visit me on the spot, and prevent a further violation of God's laws. But it
came not. I then felt that all was over, and that
I might go on and fill up the cup of wrath ; as I
had gone, according to my own judgment, too far
to be recalled. From that time I became worse
than I had been before ; so that the passage re
corded in Matthew xii., 43, 44, was in a measure fulfilled in me, for it seemed that when the
unclean spirit returned, he was stronger than before. Thus I continued for some months, till the
Lord, in the abundance of his mercy, brought me
to the port of Boston. I was there pretty roughly
handled by *old Alcohol*, spent all my wages, and
left it again in debt, (as usual,) taking with me for a
sea stock, one gallon of gin, and two pounds of tobacco. I was bound to Malaga, in the brig Byron,
of Boston, and on the voyage I began to feel it
necessary that I should do something towards
ameliorating my own condition. Other men were
possessed of good clothes, and I was almost desti
tute. Some spoke of home and happy friends, but
mine were far from me. I had separated myself
from them by bad conduct, and saw no hope of
again beholding their cheering countenances, while
I continued in the course I was then pursuing.
And what appeared still worse to me was, that my
shipmates could lie down (as far as I could judge)

in perfect tranquillity, while my mind was tortured with the thoughts of death and hell. While others slept I wept over sin, and tried to pray. But alas! I could not. My mind, in the midst of my tears, was filled with *curses and blasphemies.* But when I arose from my slumbers and resumed my duties, while my mind was engaged in other things, I had a little peace, which remained only as long as my thoughts were turned on my duty: that done, I was again troubled concerning my soul. To appease my conscience, my Bible was again brought from the bottom of my chest, where, by some strange fatality, I always found it when I wished to refer to it. From these frequent stirrings I inferred that I must do something towards my own salvation. Like every sinner, when first awakened by a sense of danger, I wanted to purchase by good works what God has said every man must receive, " without money and without price."

A FOREMAST HAND.

To be continued.

THE SAILOR.

" PRAY for the sailor—pray for him
　While tossing on the deep,
That harmlessly the raging storm
　May round his vessel sweep.

" When clouds o'erhang the wintry sky,
　And howls the tempest loud,
Pray that the angry billows may
　Not be the sailor's shroud.

' Pray for his safety and return,
　Some humble cot to cheer,
Where hearts with pain and anguish burn
　In every storm's career.

Pray for the sailor—that his soul,
  When all his toils are o'er,
In heaven be safely moored at last,
  To live for evermore."

Sailor's Magazine.

------~~~~~------

INCIDENTS IN A SAILOR'S LIFE.

ADDRESSED TO SEAMEN. (*Continued.*)

Lafayette College, May 17, 1843

I had read in the word of God, if "any one is
afflicted among you, let him pray. Is any merry?
let him sing psalms." I therefore had recourse
to my prayer-book, and learned the 100th Psalm,
which I attempted to use as a substitute for the
songs I had been wont to sing in my leisure hours.
I often sung it with tears in my eyes; but it did
not make me holy. My heart was hard as ada-
mant still. Finding that this course availed me
nothing, I resolved to board in a *Sailor's Home*
when the vessel arrived in Boston, thinking that
if I lived with respectable people, I should be
ashamed to act otherwise than they did. In short,
I desired a change in my ways, and yet could not
let go the world. This too I found to be "vanity
and vexation of spirit." However, on the 9th of
January, 1841, the Lord brought me again to
Boston, and as soon as the vessel was made fast,
I took my clothes to the Sailor's Home, on Fort
Hill, was introduced to the landlord, and by him
ushered to the *reading-room*. I sat down on the
chair nearest to the door, and began to reconnoi-
tre. The first conclusion I came to (after glancing

around the room at the boarders,) was that I had no business there, unless I could appear as decent and respectable as they were. At that time I had not a *jacket* to my back. I therefore resolved immediately that I would become sober and careful; but resolutions based on so frail a foundation as self, were held inviolate no longer than till some one tempted me to break them. One resolution to abstain from ardent spirits I kept a *whole hour ;* another five days; but on the sixth was tempted by a female to drink, and had not sufficient moral courage to say, No! and consequently broke my promise.

Oh! that the ladies knew the influence they have over the mind of the sailor, and would use that influence for good! The following are some. of the reasons why I broke my resolutions: I kept the company of those persons who were in the habit of using the "POISON." I visited with them the theatre, dance-house, circus and rum-shop, and was therefore continually in the midst of temptation, which, when resisted, laid me open to the taunts and jeers of my companions, which I could not stand without divine help. I drank nothing but cider, it is true, yet that led me in the way of, and increased my desire for something stronger. Breaking my resolutions thus, from time to time, I felt that it was useless to make any more, as it was but lying continually. With this view of my own frailty and weakness, instead of renewing my determination to become temperate, and seeking help from on high, I (on the contrary), gave way with reckless stupidity to the cravings of my insatiable thirst, and determined to try to reform no more; but to resume my former way of living. But "God's ways are not as our ways, nor his thoughts as our thoughts," or he had left me to myself to fill up the " cup of wrath against the day of wrath." God, who is rich in mercy, dealt not with me as I deserved. He did not suffer me to follow the dictates of my own sinful heart. He saw me give up to sinful pleasures, and his bowels of compassion were open to me. He stretched forth his hand, and plucked me from the brink of eternal death.

The week had been spent in revellings and drunkenness. The theatre was preferred to the prayer-meeting, and Sabbath morning found me as reckless and impenitent as before. On that morning (the 17th,) the landlord, (Capt. Buffun,) came into the reading-room, where I was sitting, and inquired who would go to church. Some of the men rose to go with him; but I sat still. He then addressed me personally, and requested me to go with him to the *Mariner's Church*. I consented, rather reluctantly, and remarked, that as it was snowing, I might as well go there as anywhere else, to while away the time till noon. I went. But so far from whiling away the time, the Lord there taught me the true value of it. The text was taken from Haggai, 1st chapter and 5th verse: " Now, therefore, thus saith the Lord of hosts : con sider your ways." And in so glaring a light was the situation of the sinner portrayed, that the truth carried an arrow of conviction to my heart, and left there a wound, for which I could find no *healing balm, no antidote*, till JESUS appeared in all his loveliness, and spoke comfort to my troubled soul by his " peace-speaking blood."

When I felt the horrors of my situation, I listened very attentively to hear of the remedy. I heard that the only way to obtain peace, was, to

give my heart and soul to Christ, without reserve
or delay. This however appeared to me to be unnecessary. I went to church again in the afternoon and evening, hoping to find some way by
which I might be saved without entirely giving up
the world. To resign my worldly pleasures was
too great a sacrifice. My shipmates would laugh
me to scorn. I could not keep their company,
and must therefore be ridiculed. All these things
were set before my mind's eye, in their most lively
colors, by the archenemy of souls.

In the evening. at the "Monthly Concert of
Prayer for SEAMEN" I heard some letters read by
the pastor, which he had received from *pious seamen*. They carried to my heart a desire to feel as
the writers profess to feel. New sensations, crowd-
ing one upon another, filled my soul with such
views of my own nothingness, as I had never before experienced.   •

I saw myself a lost, ruined, guilty, and depraved worm of the dust, to whom nothing remained in justice to my former life, but the black-
ness of darkness ; and if any thing could increase
the astonishment I felt at the long-suffering and
forbearing mercy of the Lord toward my guilty
soul, it was the scene which followed the reading
of the letters. 'I saw with surprise several respect-
able-looking seamen in different parts of the house,
rise, and declare their allegiance to the King of
kings, and claim him as " the Lord of their righteousness." They told of deliverance from hell
and the grave, through the merits of the Redeemer
They spoke of the joy arising from a sense of par
doned sin, and the happiness experienced while
under the shadow of the Almighty's wing.

Here new wonders burst in upon my soul ; it

shrunk from itself; desired to look up, but dared not, so great was the mountain of sins. A sailor pious! It was to me a miracle. I loathed myself. Death stared me in the face, as my just deserts. The horrors of a broken law appalled my guilty soul. I saw myself condemned, and acknowledged my sentence just.

When the services were closed, I returned home, and crept to my bed almost in despair. I would willingly have prayed before retiring, but the fear of man prevented me. As willingly would I have eased my mind with promises of the future; but conscience said that it would not heal the past. I would have slept, but I could not. I desired to banish from my thoughts both of the past and of the future; but the arrow of conviction rankled in the newly opened wound, and set both peace and rest at defiance. In that dread hour, while suffering the excruciating agonies of a tortured mind, and writhing under the influence of dark despair—then came Satan, to goad my already burdened conscience by casting up the mountains of my sins, which appeared to separate me from the only one to whom I could look for pardon and peace. The following were a few of the most impassable, my conception of God being so poor and limited: "You are too late now. You have sinned away your day of grace; to pray is useless! You cannot be forgiven." All this I felt inclined to believe. The offers of mercy I had rejected, the neglected morning and evening worship, and the prayer-meetings at the Home, that I had refused to attend; also the theatre I had chosen in its stead, all rose up against me in dread array, and awakened within me a desire to serve God with all my heart. I accordingly requested a friend to call me early in the morning, that I might attend the family worship. I arose before daylight in the morning, and descended to the reading-room. On entering, I perceived by the light of the lamp, that the Bible was open. A thought immediately darted across my mind, that some passage in that good book would convey peace to my troubled soul. I read, and the following words solemnly impressed my mind. "Saul, Saul, why persecutest thou me?" I burst into a flood of tears, and felt truly, "that it was hard to kick against the pricks." I turned to the person who was in the room with me, and said, "Mr. Hall, I have need of the same power that converted Saul, to bring my soul from the path of destruction."

He conversed with me some time on the subject of religion, but without the desired effect. He pointed me to the "Lamb of God, that taketh away the sins of the world;" but my heart was not sufficiently subdued to cast off the world entirely. The wound was not sufficiently deep to induce me to seek the true balm of Gilead. After breakfast, with my mind in this perturbed state, I left the house, to seek in other scenes some change of feeling, something to alleviate the pains and quench the fires that with indomitable fury burned within. Just as well might I have striven to fly from self and seek utter annihilation, as to fly from either the Spirit or the presence of God.

A FOREMAST HAND.

To be continued.

'MY SPIRIT SHALL NOT ALWAYS STRIVE'
GEN. VI. 3.

" SAY, sinner, hath a voice within,
    Oft whisper'd to thy secret soul,
Urg'd thee to leave the ways of sin,
    And yield thy heart to God's control ?

" Hath something met thee in the path
    Of worldliness and vanity,
And pointed to the coming wrath,
    And warned thee from that wrath to flee ?

: Sinner, it was a heavenly voice,
    It was the Spirit's gracious call,
I. bade thee make the better choice,
    And haste to seek in Christ thine all.

" Spurn not the call to life and light;
    Regard in time the warning kind;
That call, thou may'st not always slight,
    And yet the grace of mercy find,

" God's Spirit will not always strive
    With harden'd, self-destroying man ;
Ye, who persist his love to grieve,
    May never hear his voice again.

" Sinner—perhaps this very day,
    Thy last accepted hour may be ;
Oh, should'st thou grieve him thus away
    Then hope may never beam on thee.

HYM.

———————

INCIDENTS IN A SAILOR'S LIFE.

ADDRESSED TO SEAMEN.   (*Continued.*)

Lafayette College, June 20, 1843.

I After leaving the house, I shaped my course
for the wharves, and strolled about among the

shipping without any fixedness of purpose; but had not wandered far when I met two of the seamen who were boarding at the Sailor's Home. One of them accosted me with, " Well, C——e, what do you say for New Orleans ?"

Without considering what I was saying or doing. I consented to go with them, and immediately proceeded to the ship. We waited a few minutes for the captain, and when he came on board, after asking a few questions concerning the wages, I signed the articles to go to New Orleans and Europe, and agreed to go on board the same afternoon at four o'clock.

On my way back to the Home I began to reflect on what I had done, and to think of my poor dear mother from whom I had been absent three years and a half. I resolved to write to her and tell her of my whereabouts, (for she knew it not, but was looking daily for my return). When I reached the Home I did so ; and while writing, my mind was racked with the fears of death and hell, which caused me to feel (and express it too) that the way of the transgressor is hard. I had a strong presentiment that I should be lost in that vessel, and felt that I richly deserved it too.

Under this impression I wrote a second letter to my mother, after which I called the landlord, and placing in his hands her address, requested him if any thing should happen to me on the passage, to secure my money and clothes, (such as they were.) and send them to my mother. so strong was my presentiment that the Lord would spare me no longer.

He promised that he would comply with my request, if necessary ; and after eyeing me for a moment with apparent concern, he arose and left

the room, beckoning me to follow him, which I did
with mingled sensations of fear and shame, for I
thought that he had taken notice of the alteration
of my conduct, and I felt almost ashamed of myself
for having manifested so much concern for my own
safety. I followed him however to a private room,
and listened to him with interest while he described the state of a soul out of Christ. I thought
my heart would burst with grief, when I saw myself just in the same condition as he had pictured
the unbeliever ; and, in the bitterness of my heart
I gave vent to a flood of tears, such as I had never
shed before. I felt myself a great criminal in the
pres nce of my offended Judge, while the sword of
justice hung over my head suspended by a hair.
I felt lost! lost!! forever. The thunders of Sinai
appeared ready to burst upon me and overwhelm
my troubled mind. I "believed and trembled."
My friend, in his eagerness to benefit my soul,
probed the wound to the quick, and then, like a
skilful physician, applied the healing balm, "the
balm of Gilead," that serves to make the wounded
whole. to melt the shackles of sin, and set the prisoner free. He told me of the Saviour and his for-
giving love, of his desire that none should perish,
but that all should inherit eternal life, and of the
sacrifice he made to purchase redemption for fallen man. These truths, beautiful as they are,
cast but a momentary gleam across my pathway,
and seemed but to render my case still more hopeless I then saw my own deformity for the first
time in its true light ; that gleam of light served
but to expose the hidden corruptions of my nature,
and having done this, left me in still greater darkness. I saw not the efficacy of the *Saviour's blooa*
to wash out such deep-stained guilt as that which

had taken possession of my soul; I therefore felt
assured that Christ would not forgive so vile a
worm of the dust. I saw myself a fit object for
God to exercise his divine wrath upon, inasmuch
as I had cast away and slighted the sure mercies
of God in Christ Jesus, and was now grasping at
that which was forever removed beyond my reach.
And "was mercy clean gone forever?" Could the
Lord forgive one who had sinned against His Most
Holy Law for twenty years?—Would he condescend to return and love ME freely? Was his
anger indeed turned away? Yes! Glorious
truth! Soul cheering assurance! "It is I, against
whom you have sinned," says the Saviour. "Be not
afraid." "I am the way, the truth, and the life."
"He that believeth on me, though he were dead,
yet shall he live." *Rise then, ye that are dead in
trespasses and sins! seamen obey the call and be saved.
He will give you life eternal.*

My friend told me that he had sinned against
the same Lord and Saviour thirty years; yet had
he been rescued from the brink of the *pit*, and that
the Saviour was willing to save me though in the
same perilous condition; that he had carried the
Redeemer to sea in his heart, and that it was not
difficult (when Jesus was on board), to endure the
scoffs and jeers of his impious shipmates.

These salutary truths seemed to inspire me with
courage, and with a desire to spend the remainder
of my days in the service of such a Master. Observing perhaps some likelihood of change in my
conduct, he, pressed upon me the necessity of seeking the Lord in my closet, and begged me to seek
counsel from my Saviour in all things, whether of
a temporal or spiritual nature. assuring me at the
same time, from the page of Holy writ, that he

would never leave or forsake me, or any other person who put their trust in him. Before leaving him I felt determined to seek the Lord and strive to serve him. I had read, when very young, the Pilgrim's Progress, by Bunyan, and its truths; many of them came into my mind, which caused a desire to read that good book again I sought to obtain a copy of it, that I might discern how far I had travelled on the road to ruin. But alas, I was only on the point of leaving the " city of Destruction," though I afterwards fell in the " Slough of Despond."

The next morning, as I was about to leave the house to go on board, (for the vessel did not sail as appointed,) my friend Captain Buffum brought me a copy of the desired work, and with it another little book called the Christian's Daily Food, and begged me to read it whenever I had an opportunity; but above all, said he, " seek Christ the sinner's friend," and hoist your colors directly when you get on board, that your shipmates may see what you intend doing, as though he had said, show them that you intend to fight under the blood-stained banner of the cross. Shortly after receiving this counsel, I left the house with a bundle of clothes under my arm, and proceeded towards the vessel. But scarce had I crossed the threshold, before my mind was filled with sadness at the thought of leaving the place which, I trust, was the birth-place of my soul unto righteousness. It was indeed a Sailor's Home to my soul. Oh, that it may prove so to many more of the tempest-tossed sons of the deep! I then remembered that I was about to leave the place which abounded in religious privileges, and cast myself among men that feared not the Lord neither sought a knowledge of

nis ways. I remembered too, that only a week pre
vious, I had been invited to the prayer-meeting in
that house, and had given the theatre the preference
and now, that I would have given worlds to have
enjoyed the privileges, I was forced to leave it, and
that too on the very day on which that prayer-meeting was to be held. I felt that I was tearing myself away from all that was dear to me in life ; and
while tears, scalding tears of contrition, coursed
their way in rapid succession down my burning
cheeks, I cast my bundle in the street, and ran
back to the house to beg an interest in their pray
ers when they met in the evening. I saw a pious
man in the doorway, and requested him to pray
for me that I might hold out as a bright and shining light on board the vessel, and be finally saved
through Christ the Redeemer. I went away somewhat relieved by the promise he made me to comply with my request, and in a few moments I was
on board and ready to sail. The crew were ordered to get breakfast. and I went below with them,
thinking that it was better for me to commence
the work of the Lord at once than to leave it undone until the ship was out at sea. I took from
my chest the Bible which had been so long buried
beneath the clothes at the bottom of it, and read,
commencing at the first chapter of Genesis.

It will perhaps be needless to tell you, my reader,
that I was laughed at. But the day in which a
blaspheming shipmate could drive me from the
word of God I trust. had already passed away. I
felt that their jeers and scoffs could not hurt me
while God was my friend ; and that their smiles,
could I gain them, would avail me nothing in the
day of judgment. And now I rejoice in the bliss
ful hope, that all such days, with their sins and in

iquities, have been forever banished from the book
of God's remembrance.

A FOREMAST HAND.

To be continued.

'AWAK'D by Sinai's awful sound,
My soul in bonds of guilt I found,
  And knew not where to go;
  Eternal truth did loud proclaim,
' The sinner must be born again,
  Or sink to endless woe.'

" When to the law I trembling fled,
  It poured its curses on my head,—
  I no relief could find;
  This fearful truth increas'd my pain,
  The sinner must be born again,'
  And whelm'd my tortured mind.

" Again did Sinai's thunders roll,
  And guilt lay heavy on my soul,
  A vast oppressive load;
  Alas! I read and saw it plain,
' The sinner must be born again,'
  Or drink the wrath of God.

" The saints I heard with rapture tell,
  How Jesus conquered Death and Hell,
  And broke the fowler's snare;
  Yet, when I found this truth remain,
' The sinner must be born again,'
  I sunk in deep despair.

" But while I thus in anguish lay,
  The gracious Saviour pass'd this way,
  And felt his pity move;
  The sinner, by his justice slain,
  Now by his grace *is* born again,
  And sings redeeming love.

                                    OCEAN

INCIDENTS IN A SAILOR'S LIFE.

ADDRESSED TO SEAMEN. (*Continued.*)

Lafayette College, July 18, 1843.

DEAR READER :—When I commenced writing this narrative for your perusal, hoping that God might be glorified and your soul benefited by it, I did not intend carrying it to so great a length. I have therefore detained you much longer than I expected when I got under weigh. However, if you will bear with me a little longer, and I can have the indulgence of our kind friend the editor, I will proceed.

I left you, or you left me, rather, last month, sitting in the forecastle of the ship Birmingham, reading my Bible. I had not read long, before one of the crew came to me, and asked me if I was religious. (Here Satan tempted me). I answered, "I am not, (here grace prevailed,) but through grace in the Lord Jesus Christ, I intend to become a Christian ; or, at least, to try it for a season : for I have served Satan twenty-two years, and have received no remuneration for my labors. I have fought long and well for him, with a zeal worthy of a better cause ; yet am I unrewarded. save by the tortures of a guilty conscience. Now is my determination settled. I will serve God, if He be my helper." My shipmate smiled, as though in doubt as to the stability of my determined resolution, and said it was well if I could " stick to it." I suffered much in my mind till towards noon, when I took from my pocket the little book (Daily Food,) given to me by brother Buffum, and read " If any man sin, we have an *Ad vocate* with the Father, even Jesus Christ, the Righteous, and He is the propitiation for our sins, and not for ours only, but for the sins of the whole world." And beneath that the following lines ;

> " He (Christ) ever lives to intercede
>   Before his Father's face,
> Give him, my soul, thy cause to plead,
>   Nor doubt a Father's grace."

Here the mystery appeared solved. I had been doubting a Father's grace; but I determined to do so no more. I stowed myself away in the be-tween-decks, among the cargo, and cried, " O.Lord ! if I must perish, let it be here, even at the foot of the cross, where never yet man perished, at the feet of a crucified Redeemer." The turbulence of my mind being somewhat allayed by this prayer, through the intercession of a Divine Mediator, I arose from my knees, and resumed my duty with more hope than before. Now, the moral gloom which had hitherto enshrouded my mind, was in a measure alleviated ; and I. began to breathe more freely, indulging a faint hope that God would, for Christ's sake, have mercy on my sin-polluted and heavy-burdened soul. But since the first rays of an eternal light had been partially unfolded to my view, I determined, with all the energies of my soul, to perish only there, feeling like Esther of old ; " If I perish, I perish."

I embraced every opportunity I could get, with-out neglecting my duty, to seek *my Bethel*, the BETHESDA OF MY SOUL, and there pour my com-plaints and sorrows into the ear of Omnipotence. Our vessel having left the wharf at Boston about 11 A. M., with a strong north-wester, by night we were well clear of the land: the watches were set

and I was chosen by the chief mate.   While pacing
the deck with my watchmates, every one had his
own peculiar yarn to spin about landlords and land-
ladies, and some began to form their plans for the
next port, or to make good promises for the future.
Alas! made only to be broken, should they fall
into the hands of the "land shark."   I joined them
in their walk, and for the first time in my life,
found that I had nothing to talk about.   Nothing,
did I say?   I had something.   I had an inex-
haustible theme.   But, the question arose, Shall
I broach it?   "No" said Satan, "they will revile
you."   "Blessed are ye when men shall revile you
for my sake," says the Saviour.   I did bring this
truth before them : "The way of transgressors is
hard," but was almost immediately overpowered
with opposing arguments; among which, that I
should prove a hypocrite in the end, was not the
least.   I now saw for the first time also, the eminent danger I was in of clinging to the world, and
found myself, at the time when I most required religious aid and instruction, afloat among a set of
men as bad as myself, and, therefore, could expect
no consolation from them.   In this crisis I flew to
him who was alone "mighty to save," nor did I
plead in vain.

Two days after leaving Boston, while sitting at
dinner in the forecastle, I heard that appalling
cry : "A man overboard."   Sailors will know what
my feelings were, for they have felt them.   But
the landsman must hear it before he can possibly
sympathize with me.   For pen cannot describe,
nor pencil delineate the horror that is depicted on
the countenance of the seaman, as he beholds his
shipmate struggling with the mighty waves of
ocean, and sees that he cannot render him any as-

sistance. I rushed on deck, and ran forward with
the rest of the crew, but alas! was only in time to
see the vessel leap upon his defenceless head, like
a beast of the forest on its prey, and the water
closed over him forever. The crew then ran aft,
hoping that he would rise again; but in vain. I ran
up to the mizen-top, and watched for him, but my
search was fruitless. While there, I prayed to
God in the anguish of my soul, for fear that I
should be the next cut off with all my sins upon
me.

In a short time after the above event, I learned
that it was a Christian duty to deny self for Christ's
sake. I therefore made way with cards, dice, song-
books, dream-books, novels, romances, tobacco, and
all intoxicating drinks, and prayed the Lord to
erase the very thoughts of them from my memory.

My shipmates now called my attention; I longed
for their conversion; I plead with them, and they
persecuted me. One, however, listened to the tale
of a Saviour's sufferings and death, and wept over
them too. He agreed with me that we should travel the heavenly pathway together; we prayed together; but scarce had we taken our departure from
the city of Destruction, before he fell into the Slough
of Despond, and in his fear came very nigh ruining
me. He turned back to the world, while I, through
grace, determined to perish (if need be) in an at-
tempt to reach the opposite shore: and I trust my
determination was not made in vain. I continued
to warn my shipmates still; but my companion declared that he had sinned against the Holy Ghost.
He thought that it was impossible for him to be
saved; and while in this disturbed state of mind,
he filled me also with apprehensions of the same
direful import. Yet in all this grace was my de-

liverer. I collected my shipmates on the forecastle on the Sabbath day, and read tracts and good books to them. But in a short time some of them cursed me for reading what they called "Christ-killing tracts," fearing (to use their own words) that the "ship would be carried to heaven in a hurry." Our good ship, notwithstanding, sped on her course ; each day bringing with it some slanderings or curses to me, on account of my religious principles. While reading my Bible, some would sit beside me, and sing some blackguard song, or relate some obscene story, to draw my mind away from the Word of God.

In the providence of God, after a passage of forty-four days, we arrived at New Orleans. But O ! how was my heart pained when forced to behold the total desecration of the Sabbath. I was horror-stricken when I saw, on that holy day, the market thronged with purchasers and salesmen, the grog-shops filled with men callous to every good and holy feeling, and giving vent to the most horrid curses and blasphemies ; and the tables surrounded with gamblers, whose souls appeared to hang upon the hazard of the die ; so intently were they engaged in their lawless pursuits. These things shocked me so that I left my vessel as soon as she was discharged, and took up my abode at the Sailor's Home, where I found several pious seamen, and after a short stay, shipped with them in a ship bound to the port of Philadelphia.

We had not been long on board before the Lord gave us one of those who sailed with us for our hire. On the 16th of May, we reached our port of destination, and on the 23d, three of my shipmates besides myself, united ourselves in an everlasting covenant with the Lamb of God in his holy

14

sanctuary, (the Mariner's Church) under the care of the Rev. O. Douglass.

Thanks to the good people of the land. tha tho sailor has now a place where he can worship his God, when his perilous voyage is ended. May the blessing of God rest upon all who have aided in this good work! is the pious sailor's prayer. It is necessary that I should say but little more. and therefore. if my reader will just "lay to" till next month, I will conclude this brief. *very brief* narrative of my life. And I hope that the memory of the writer and the patience of the reader may not have been taxed in vain.

A FOREMAST HAND.

To be continued.

MY SAILOR BOY.

BY MARY S. B. DANA.

" THE storm is loud, the waves run high,
And clouds have darkened all the sky;
O God! my heart is full of grief,
Now hear my prayer and send relief;
If thou but whisper, ' Peace, be still,'
The winds and waves obey thy will;
Thou art the source of every joy :—
O God! protect my sailor boy!

" When storms arise, how can I sleep?
My sailor boy is on the deep!
I know thy never sleeping eye,
Great God! is watching from on high:
Thou only canst the storm control,
On this I'll rest my troubled soul;
Thou art the source of every joy :—
O God! protect my sailor boy!

' Amid the tempest's awful roar,
Great God! the sailor feels thy power;
When ocean storms shall cease to rage,
Still may thy power his thoughts engage,

From every refuge may he flee
Till he has made a friend of THEE:
Thou art the source of every joy:
O God! protect my sailor boy!

" My Father, shall I ask in vain?
Wilt thou my humble prayers disdain?
O no! thy kind Almighty arm
Will keep my sailor boy from harm;
I know thou'lt hear my earnest plea,
I'll leave my sailor boy with thee;
O God! thou source of every joy,
Protect and save my sailor boy!

Charleston, May 31, 1843.   *Sailor's Magazine.*

INCIDENTS IN A SAILOR'S LIFE.

ADDRESSED TO SEAMEN.   (*Concluded.*)

Lafyette College, August 17, 1834.

A FEW weeks after I joined the Mariner's Church,
I shipped, together with two other seamen, on
board the schooner R——c, bound to Santa Cruz,
in the West Indies; but previous to signing the
articles, we requested the captain to allow us time
for prayer, to which he consented, although not a
professor of religion.   On that voyage there was
heard no cursing in the forecastle, neither was
there any rum drank there.   I cannot say as much
of the after end of the vessel.   The captain would
rip out an oath sometimes, and the mate also.   On
one occasion the captain, after having given way
to his spleen in a burst of profanity, turned to a
pious sailor who was standing at the wheel, and
remarked that he had been enabled to leave off
swearing, in some measure, since we came on board
his vessel; and that he hoped to be entirely cured

before he parted with us: the same influence, I trust, governed the remainder of the crew. As soon as we arrived at Santa Cruz, I sought out the church, and found many of the friends of Christ, who invited me to bring my shipmates on shore to visit them on their plantations, (for the most of them were planters,) and sent their carriage to the wharf in the evening, to convey us to them as soon as the labors of the day were over. I then saw that the sailor was respected, and longed for the day to arrive, when all the sons of the Great Deep shall be known in foreign lands as the "Sons of God."

One of the planters whom we visited, had converted his *still-room* into a *school-room;* had banished alchohol from his premises, and given all his slaves one day in the week to dispose of their produce, so that they might keep holy the Sabbath day to the Lord. He called his slaves together, and requested us to address them, which we willingly did for Christ's sake. On the whole, our company was *sought*, rather than *shunned*, by the most influential persons on the Island. I have not made mention of this for the purpose of taking the glory to ourselves: but to set forth the goodness of God, as well as to show that the sailor will soon be lifted up from the level of the brute creation (where the intoxicating bowl and the "strange woman" have brought him), to that of mediocrity at least. And the sailor's energetic spirit will not suffer him to stop there, but will cause him to aspire even higher among the inhabitants of the civilized globe. In this, too, the mercy of our God is strikingly manifest. even in the stretching of his hand to those who had so long been neglected and given up of men.

While lying there, I was deeply impressed with the belief, that it was my duty to prepare for the holy ministry. This, at first sight, appeared a task altogether impossible. I had spent all my money in " riotous living," and was therefore unwilling to indulge a hope, that I should ever attain to so high and holy an office ; still the same feelings seemed to pervade my mind night and day, and gave me no rest. Sometimes I imagined that it was the workings of the evil one, making me desirous of being seen in the world, and I prayed the Lord to drive such thoughts away from me, and let them perish where they had their birth, unless they were sent from on high, to spur me forward in my duty ; and if the latter was the case, that he would point out a way for the accomplishment of what appeared to me so gigantic an undertaking.

After some struggles on my part, I came to the determination to adopt the following resolutions, viz. : first, that I would make it the subject of earnest prayer ; and secondly, that I would not seek it myself, lest I should be seeking material to feed my own ambition and self-esteem. I began to carry out these resolutions ; and on one occasion, after reading a tract pertaining somewhat to the subject which had been engrossing my mind so long, I felt a powerful visitation of the Spirit of God. I fell upon my knees, but was speechless for some seconds at the thought of my own unworthiness, and God's abundant goodness. At length the power of speech returned, and my soul was drawn out in prayer, after which I arose from my knees in full assurance that I should one day be permitted to stand between the living and the dead, and proclaim the glad news of salvation through a Redeemer. I continued in prayer for special guid

14*

ance in this affair all the passage from Santa Cruz
to Philadelphia, and on my arrival I jumped into
the boat, and went ashore with the captain before the vessel had time to haul into the wharf.
Directly I landed, I left the boat and ran up to
the Sailor's Home, and from that to my pastor's
house, where, before twenty minutes had elapsed,
sufficient was said to prove to me that the way was
opened for me to prepare for the holy ministry,
without any seeking on my part whatever. To
the Rev. O. Douglass, pastor of the Mariner's
Church, Philadelphia, (through grace,) I am deeply
indebted for the privilege which I now enjoy—
even that of preparing to become a laborer in the
vineyard of the Lord ; my highest aim now is to
spend the remaining days of my pilgrimage on the
earth in the service of the Lord, in such a manner
as he may deem most subservient to the spreading
of the Gospel of Christ among the long-neglected
sons of the great deep.

Now, my readers, since you have been shown in
this brief narrative of facts, a few of the wondrous
dealings of the Lord with one of the most unworthy of his rebellious creatures, see if you cannot,
from the commencement of my course until this
hour, trace the finger of Omnipotence in every step
that has been taken. Surely you can ! and will
say with me, " This is the Lord's doing, and it is
marvellous in our eyes."

A few words with you, and I have done. Have
you found the " pearl of great price ?" Have you
chosen the " good part that cannot be taken away ?"
Do you love the Saviour, and delight in his glori
ous Gospel ? If you can answer these questions
in the affirmative, 'tis well ! press towards the mark
for the prize, bearing in mind that it is at the end

of the race. If not; oh, "seek the Saviour new while he may be found; and call upon him while he is near!" For, rest assured that, whoever you may be, and whatever your occupation in this world, you are not excluded from the law of God, nor, if you break that law, will you be excluded from its punishment hereafter.

Now, a word to the sailor who is yet in the gall of bitterness and bond of iniquity; who is still tossed about on life's troubled ocean, without a hope to buoy up his soul when the final storm of God's wrath shall break upon our guilty world.

If this should meet the eye of such an one (as I hope it will), to him I would say, Shipmate! you and I are bound on the voyage of life; we are sailing fast to the shores of eternity, and are daily drawing nearer to our port. You have a precious and immortal soul as well as myself,— a soul that must live even after the sun has refused to shed his glorious light, and every star in the bright firmament of heaven is blasted out. When the things of earth have every one sunk into oblivion, your soul and mine will both be sensitive, either of the bliss of heaven, or the excruciating tortures of a guilty conscience in the shades of endless woe. Which condition will entirely depend on the course they steer while here in a probationary state. Think you, that while you keep your helm up, and steer broad off for the gulf of perdition,—while you continue to drive carelessly on, and let the treacherous stream hurry you to the whirlpool of despair,—while you are reproaching and reviling the more cautious mariner, who, having discovered his danger, and prudently hauled his wind, may now be seen cautiously standing in for the head lands of hope, with the cross of Christ for his guid

ing star, the Saviour for his pilot, and the Bible
for his chart—that you can be happy? 'Tis impossible! Look around you, my friend, and you
will find, that while you are nearing destruction's
dangerous brink, some of the very persons who
were of your convoy, are even now spreading
the sails of their affections to catch the breeze of
divine grace, that they may be wafted towards the
haven of eternal rest.

The same privileges await you—the same breezes
invite you to those celestial abodes of everlasting
bliss. Say, then! will you any longer delay? will
you stand on, in spite of the warnings of God's
word, and the admonitions of kind friends, and
make shipwreck of your precious and immortal
soul, rather than anchor forever in the calm ocean
of God's love? If you will, I beg you to remember that, " He that is often reproved, and harden-
eth his neck ; shall suddenly be destroyed, and that
without remedy." " The wicked shall be turned
into hell, and all the nations that forget God."
Oh, my friend! take the advice of one whose experience has made him acquainted with your extreme danger. Oh! delay not another moment ;
but down with your helm instantly. Heave about
you quick, while you have sea-room ; for, if you
miss stays, your destruction will be inevitable—you
must be irretrievably and irrecoverably lost. How
will you decide? Time speeds on his course, and
there is but one alternative, heaven or hell—happiness or woe! Choose before it be everlastingly
too late. Oh, let me entreat you to embrace the
opportunity now, while the angels of heaven are
waiting to convey the glad tidings to the throne,
that another sinner has been reclaimed—that another soul has been redeemed from the galling

yoke of sin.   I could bring you a whole cargo of
reasons why you should cling to the cross now,
but sufficient has been said already to tire your
patience, I am afraid.   I will, therefore, close by
saying, if you refuse the heavenly message, and
are lost, you cannot say that your blood is on the
skirts of my garment.   Farewell!   Let us "strive"
to meet each other on the shores of the heavenly
Canaan, where we may dwell forever with our blessed Redeemer, for his name's sake.   Amen.

A FOREMAST HAND

THE PRISONER'S ADDRESS TO HIS MOTHER.

"I'VE wandered far from thee, mother,
    Far from our happy home;
I've left the land that gave me birth,
    In other climes to roam;
And Time, since then, has rolled his years,
    And marked them on my brow;
Yet still I often thought of thee,—
    I'm thinking of thee now.

"I'm thinking of those days, mother,
    When with such earnest pride,
You watched the dawnings of my youth,
    And pressed me to your side;
Then love had filled my trusting heart
    With hopes of future joy,
And thy bright fancy honors wove
    To deck thy 'darling boy.'

'I'm thinking on the day, mother,
    I left thy watchful care,
When thy fond heart was lifted up
    To heaven—thy trust was there;
And memory brings thy parting words,
    When tears fell o'er thy cheek;
But thy last, loving, anxious look
    Told more than words could speak.

" I'm far away from thee, mother,
  No friend is near me now,
To soothe me with a tender word,
  Nor cool my burning brow ;
The dearest ties affection wove
  Are all now torn from me ;
They left me when the trouble came,
  They did not love like thee.

" I would not have thee know, mother,
  How brightest hopes decay,—
The tempter with his baneful cup,
  Has dashed them all away :
And shame has left his venomed sting
  To rack with anguish wild !
'Twould grieve thy tender breast to know
  The sorrows of thy child !

" I'm lonely and forsaken now,
  Unpitied and unblest ;
Yet still I would not have thee know
  H ow sadly I'm distressed ;
I know thou wouldst not chide me,
  Thou wouldst not give me pain,
But cheer me with thy softest words,
  And bid me hope again.

" I know thy tender heart, mother,
  Still beats as warm for me,
As when I left thee long ago,
  To cross the broad blue sea ;
And I love thee just the same, mother.
  And I long to hear thee speak,
And feel again thy balmy breath
  Upon thy care-worn cheek.

" But ah ! there is a thought, mother,
  Pervades my beating breast,
That thy free spirit may have flown
  To its eternal rest ;
And as I wipe the tear away,
  There whispers in my ear,
A voice that speaks of heaven and thee,
  And bids me seek thee there."

Washington, Jan 6, 1847.   G. H.

THE SAILOR KNEELING BY HIS CHEST.

" THE captain of the brig Ceres related the fol·
lowing interesting fact. One of the apprentices
on board of my vessel, a youth of bad character
for swearing and profaning the name of God, after
reading a tract called 'Serious thoughts on Eter·
nity,' was observed several days by the mate to be
very thoughtful and serious, and sighed at times
as if something lay heavy on his mind. The mate
asked him what caused him to look so sorrowful?
'Ah! Mr. ———, eternity! eternity! that awful
word rings in my ears all day, and all night too.
What will become of me in eternity?' The mate
observed, he was but a poor hand to speak to the
lad on religious feelings, being but very little ac·
quainted with them; but said, ' You have been a
wicked lad; but if you pray to God he may have
mercy. Do your duty, and refrain from swearing;
and read good books, and particularly the Bible.'
He would, after this, often be seen, when ship's
duty did not interfere, leaning over the gunwale
of the vessel, evidently at prayer. The scoffs and
jeers of the men, on account of his seriousness and
dejection, and when reading the Bible, would not
shake him from his stability.

" He had a soul to be saved; the work was of
God; and by the assistance of his Holy Spirit, he
bore all, determined to secure an earnest of a bliss·
ful eternity. On one occasion, seeking to avoid the
scoffs of the crew, he crept. (as he thought, unper
ceived.) down the fore-hatch, and knelt down lean
ing over the chest of one of the men in prayer.
The man to whom the chest belonged, having seen
him, as he said, go down with a suspicious appear
ance, waited a few seconds, followed him, and see

ing him by his chest, dragged him on deck, and with oaths, declared he was opening his chest to rob him. The boy denied the accusation. The bustle this contest caused brought the mate forward to inquire the reason. The man accused ; the boy denied. The mate, feeling in favor of the lad, and supposing some religious cause for his being thus found, encouraged him to explain. The boy, bursting into tears, answered, ' I was trying to do what my accuser ought to do ; *I was kneeling against his chest in prayer.*' The man was so struck by the boy's manner of confession, and the sincerity of his looks, that he replied in a softened tone, ' Why did you not say so at first ?' ' Because,' the boy answered, ' I thought you would sneer and ridicule me.' ' No, far from it, I will never ridicule you again ; and will, as far as I can, prevent your being so. I sincerely believe you innocent ; and when you pray again, *remember me.* The boy continued to hold fast his faith ; he stood firm in his religious profession ; and, on his return from his voyage, became a member of a Christian church in the west of England : and to this day, appears to adorn the profession he makes, devoting his best services to promote the glory of God."

Liverpool.

EXTRACT FROM A CAPTAIN'S DIARY.

" LEFT port on the 19th of August. 30th. Commenced social worship on board in the evenings, passage out—passage homeward, morning and evening. On the Sabbath day, the morning and evening sacrifices were offered up, and divine service

performed in the cabin in the afternoon, after the
usual manner on shore.   In the gale of the 28th,
when danger threatened us on every side, and
death was evidently near to us, our God wrought
wonderfully for us, sparing our justly forfeited
lives, with the exception of one of our crew ; teach-
ing us a solemn lesson—' Be ye also ready.'

" Sept. 6th.—Was informed one of the crew was
under deep conviction, and had been in tears all
night.   I observed the next day he appeared
very thoughtful, and his mind seemed softened
with grief,—previous to this he was an awful profane swearer, and had not heard a prayer, or been
inside a meeting-house for ten years.   Judged it
most prudent not to be too urgent in this affair, but
rather to wait the issue, bearing in mind the words
of Gamaliel—' Let this work alone, if it be of God,
it will assuredly stand.'   In the evening, brought
into view the prodigal son, setting forth the exceeding love and tender compassion of God our
Saviour towards perishing sinners, who no sooner
perceives the least relenting on the sinner's part,
but he runs to meet him.   The next day com-
mented on first part of Luke, 15th, and thus continued from time to time, introducing some por-
tions of Scripture, as I thought (by the grace of
God assisting), might be most proper on this occasion.

" Sept. 9th.—Opened a conference or free-meet-
ing to be continued weekly, for all who chose to take
part in the exercises.   Acts 12th, was read as an
introduction, showing the efficacy of prayer for Peter while in prison ; offered a petition to the throne
of grace, and left the meeting open.   One old
sailor, who owned and acknowledged the brig to
have been his spiritual birth-place, spoke freely of

15

the love of God and of his hope in Christ, only la
menting how unprofitable a servant he had been,
and how barren he still was; but hoped that the in-
stitution of this meeting would be profitable to his
soul. Another sailor then rose and spoke of the
goodness of God in taking his feet from the horrible
pit, and miry clay, and placing them upon the Rock
Christ—praised his holy name for giving him so
comfortable an assurance of his acceptance in Christ,
and more particularly for casting his lot in a vessel
where these things were attended to. One of the
officers next rose, rejoicing in hope. praising God
for his goodness to one who had resisted the influence of the Spirit with all his might, but was now
forced to bow to the sceptre of King Jesus:—he
then concluded with prayer. The hymn, 'Lord
dismiss us with thy blessing,' was then sung, and
the meeting closed with the apostolic benediction.
The meeting to me was highly interesting, and
there appeared a very great attention at all times
to the religious exercises. As it respects the sailor
under conviction, I inquired of one of his shipmates (a pious sailor) what was his opinion as to
his conduct in private; he answered me that the
man seemed to be wrestling with God in prayer
for mercy. Doddridge's 'Rise and Progress of
Religion in the Soul.' was given him to read, which
he read through; a Bible and Seaman's Devotional
Assistant were given him, and he employed all his
spare moments in searching the Scriptures of truth.
Thus far he has continued steadfast, and appears
to have taken a decided stand in the cause and interest of the blessed Redeemer. Our conference
meetings were hailed with delight, and were peculiarly interesting: our Sabbaths were quiet Sab
baths, and it did appear as if the Lord frequently

met with us and smiled upon our feeble efforts. The signs of the times indicate that the Lord has already commenced a great work among us; his Spirit is striving with us, and may we not humbly rely on his promise. that in due time the abun dance of the sea shall be converted unto God?"

> " E'er since by faith I saw the stream
>   Thy flowing wounds supply,
>   Redeeming love, has been my theme,
>   And shall be when I die."

T. S.

THE FIRST BETHEL ON THE LAKES.

FROM THE LOG-BOOK OF ONE WHO HAS BEEN A SAILOR.

" It was a beautiful autumnal Sabbath morn, in 1830—not a cloud moved across the blue vault of heaven,—the tranquil waters of Ontario lay undimpled and unmoved. for all was calm and peaceful. Sweet was the silence of that holy morning —it was a type of that *heavenly rest!*

" The sun came out of his chamber in the east, rejoicing as a bridegroom to run his race, and as is customary on shipboard, the colors of the shipping were hoisted at that hour. *What is that flag yonder?* It bears a strange emblem! Inquiries were made by many, but few could satisfactorily answer. The Sabbath-school children observed it as they went to their morning school, and wondered. It was a novel thing to all, and all were surprised. It was not worn by a stranger's vessel. *She was well known.* The silent air refused also to lift the folds of the flag, and what might be upon it was not *fully* seen. But at length the gentle breeze threw out the beautiful banner. It bore on its

chaste white ground *a dove,* having in its mouth, as
Scripture beautifully says, ' *an olive leaf plucked off,*'
and the cheering inscription, ' BETHEL !'   How
sweet is the retrospect of that morning.   How
good *God was* to let that happy ensign be unfurled
under such circumstances.   How did the heart *gush*
with hope of better times, and how delightful it
was to go away and thank the God of Bethel for
such a token of mercy !

  " The day passed on, and just at eventide the
multitude flocked to the vessel's side.   Three
schooners were laid abreast of each other, which,
with the adjacent extensive wharf, were crowded
with persons of all ages.   A solemn pause ensued !
Angels looked down, *and God looked down,* and the
hearts of the pious looked up, and met their gaze
by faith.   The silence was broken by that cheering seamen's hymn, each stanza ending with

' Sailor ! there's *hope* for the.'

The strains passed away, but not without effect,
for they called tears to many a furrowed cheek of
landsman and seaman.   Prayer was offered and
exhortation given, and the Bethel meeting on
board 'the Winnebago'—*the first on the western in-
land waters*—has never been forgotten.   Great
mercies have since descended upon seamen, and
well may it be said of Lake Ontario—' *The voice of
the Lord is upon the waters.'*   I. T. M."

- - ‑‑‑‑‑‑

A CHRISTIAN.

A CHRISTIAN is one who is snatched as a brand
from the burning, the flames of hell are quenched

in the Redeemer's blood : he is grafted into the
living vine; because it lives, *he* lives also, deriving
from the union strength and nourishment; he becomes a fruitful bough by the wells of salvation,
whose branches, thick with clusters of good fruits,
adorn the wall of God's house.—Are you, reader,
a fruitful branch in this living vine ? do you know
what this union means ? if so, happy are you.
Study to show forth the praises of Him who hath
thus had mercy on you ; but remember, that on
those who know not the nature of this union, God
will rain storms, fire and brimstone, and a horrible
tempest—this shall be the portion of their cup.
But, oh! fly sinner, fly to the Lamb of God; he
taketh away the sin of the world. Come guilty,
come needy, come just as you are. 'All the fitness
he requireth, is to feel your need of him!' . Come
now in this accepted time, and be assured he will
*n no*wise cast you out."

A SAILOR'S PRAYER.

" FATHER, the storm is loud!
   No light beams on our way,
Save when o'er yonder cloud
   The fearful lightnings play.
The frowning heavens above!
   The yawning deeps below !
Far, FAR are those we love;
   Where can the sailor go ?

" Father, to thee we turn!
   God of the earth and sea !
When sad our bosoms yearn,
   Our fears are known to thee!
Oh ! let thine eye of love
   Beam through the angry storm,
And hope sent from above,
   Appear in dove-like form !

15*

" Thy breath can 'calm the sea,
  Thy voice, the tempest's rage,
So can thy PEACE within
  Our rising fears assuage.
Father, to thee we cry !
  God of the earth and sea !
No other aid is nigh—
  Our hopes repose on thee !"

Chris. Obs.   C. M A.

THE UNSATISFYING NATURE OF WORLDLY GOOD.

" Vanity of vanities saith the preacher, vanity of vanities ; all is
vanity.—ECCLES. 1. 2.

" ECCLESIASTES is the Greek title of the book ;
the title which it bears in the Septuagint.   It sig-
nifies, THE PREACHER.   The Hebrew word for
which it is used, means, one who assembles, or
gathers the people together; and the translation
of it by the term *Ecclesiastes,* shows that the Greek
translators understood the object of the assem-
bling to be, the communication of public instruction.

" The preacher was the 'Son of David.'   To
him had been addressed, by his pious and affectionate father, the solemn charge, equally melting
and alarming : 'And thou, Solomon my son, know
thou the God of thy father, and serve him with a
perfect heart, and with a willing mind ; for the
Lord searcheth all hearts, and understandeth all
the imaginations of the thoughts : If thou seek
him he will be found of thee ; but if thou forsake
him, he will cast thee off forever.'   It was in opposition to this paternal counsel that he had gone
astray ; and possibly the tender recollection of it,
brought home to the heart by the events of Provi

dance, might be part of the means of 'restoring his soul, and making him to walk again in the paths of righteousness.'

"'The preacher' was also 'King of Jerusalem. It was the God of Israel who had chosen and ex·alted him to this dignity : but he had been guilty of forgetting and ill-requiting the Author of his greatness. As 'King of Jerusalem' he was placed in a situation, which brought within his reach 'whatsoever his soul lusted after,' and thus enabled him, in the most favorable circumstances, and on the most extensive scale, to try his infatuated ex·periments on human happiness ;—experiments, of which the great general result is expressed, with comprehensive brevity, and deep-felt emphasis, in the language already quoted,—

' *Vanity of vanities, saith the preacher, vanity of vanities ; all is vanity.*'

" This is the text of the preacher's sermon , the leading proposition, which it is his object to illus-trate and to establish, in the whole of the subse-quent part of this book,—of which he never loses sight ; which meets us, in the way of direct allu-sion, at every step and turn of the progress of his argument.

" To enter into any detached and general illus-tration of this verse, would, therefore, be to antici-pate the contents of the book. The following re-marks may be worthy of attention :—

" *In the first place.* It is to be considered as the affecting result of Solomon's own experience. He had entered into the spirit of universal inquiry, ' Who will show us any good ?' and had made the trial of the various sources of worldly happiness. He had repaired in person to the different springs, determined to take nothing upon the reported ex

perience of others, but to taste the waters for himself. He had drunk freely of them all; and in
this treatise, he describes their respective proper-
ties and virtues.—The book might, therefore. with
sufficient appropriateness, be entitled 'THE EXPE-
RIENCE OF SOLOMON.'

" *Secondly.* We are not to understand it as the
language of a mind soured and fretted by dis-
appointment,—the verdict of a morose and discon-
tented cynic, the incessant frustration of whose
hopes and desires had made him renounce the
world in disgust, while his heart was yet un-
changed, and continued secretly to hanker after the
same enjoyments; or of a wasted sensualist, who,
having run his career of pleasure, félt himself·in
capable of any longer actually enjoying what still,
however, engrossed his peevish and unavailing
wishes ; but we are to regard it as the conclusion
come to by one who had felt the bitterness of a
course of sin, and the emptiness of this world's
joys, and having been reclaimed from the 'error of
his way,' having renounced and wept over his follies, was more than ever satisfied that the 'fear ot
the Lord is wisdom,' and that ' the ways of wisdom
are the only ways of pleasantness, and her paths
alone the paths of peace.'

" *Thirdly.* Neither must we conceive him to af-
firm, in these words, that there is *no good whatever*,
no kind of enjoyment, no degree of happiness, to
be derived from the things of the world, when
they are kept in their own place, estimated on
right principles, and used in a proper manner.—
Sentiments widely different from any thing so as-
cetic and enthusiastic as this, will repeatedly come
in our way in the course of the book.—The words
before us are to be interpreted of every thing in

this world when pursued as *the portion* of him who seeks it,—when considered as constituting *the hap-piness* of a rational, immortal, and accountable being. His verdict is, that to such a creature they can yield, by themselves, no genuine and worthy satisfaction ; and that, whilst they are, in their own nature, unsatisfying even in this world, they are worse, infinitely worse than profitless, in the world to come. On this ground it is, that he pronounces them *vanity ;*—he had weighed them all in the balances, and had found them wanting.

"*Fourthly* The peculiar emphasis may be remarked with which this verdict is expressed. He does not merely say, all things are *vain :*—but ' all is *vanity ;*'—vanity itself, and *vanity of vanities ;* that is, the greatest vanity,—sheer, perfect vanity. —And he doubles the emphatic asseveration, ' Vanity of vanities ; vanity of vanities ; all is vanity.'—This shows, first, the strength of the impression on his own mind. It is not the language of a judgment hesitating between two opinions, or of a heart lingering between opposite desires ; but of a mind thoroughly made up, of a heart loathing itself for having ever for a moment yielded to a different sentiment, of decided conviction, of powerful experimental feeling.—It was a lesson which he himself had learned by the bitterest experience ; and he is anxious to prevent others from learning it in the same way. He wishes them to take his word for it ; not to venture after him in a repetition of the sad experiments on which this conclusion was founded ; but to enter directly on another course ; to seek immediately and earnestly a better portion,—even the ' peace of them that love God's law,'—the ' life' that lies in the ' Divine favor.'—the joys and the hopes of true religion.

"They are the best qualified to pronounce on the vanity and emptiness of the world, who have themselves tried it in all its forms and modes of enjoyment. Solomon made the experiment, and he 'found it wanting.' When, through Divine mercy, he 'came to himself,' he renounced the world, as 'vanity, and a thing of nought.' With penitential shame and sorrow, he returned to God, from whom he had so miserably revolted,—even to 'the fountain of living waters,'—and found Him an all-satisfying portion, peace and rest, and 'fulness of joy,'—and, in the keeping of his command-ments, 'a great reward;' and such has been the experience, the feelingly-recorded experience, of many a one besides the royal preacher. The in-sufficiency and vanity, indeed, of earthly things, as the portion of an intellectual, moral, and immortal being, ought to be held as a self-evident truth, un-susceptible of controversy, and requiring no proof. Yet, alas! what cause have we to remark in the next place ; What an affecting evidence it is of the infatuation and depravity of mankind, that neither the plainness of the truth, nor the uniformity of the experience of successive generations, produces any alteration whatever on their general conduct. Men who have made trial of the world, and have afterwards turned from it unto God, have attested, from their personal experience, its universal vanity, and, at the same time, the substantial and sat-isfactory excellence of the blessings they have chosen in its stead ;—and many a time from others have the fearful solemnities of a death-bed, and a near view of eternity, drawn forth the reluctant confession of the same truth ; a truth unheeded in the midst of life, and business, and prosperity, but brought home to the mind with dreadful certainty, when death has placed the sinner on the verge of the world to come. Yet, in despite of all this, men continue to pursue the same course. They persist in following the world with all avidity, under one or other of its various forms of falsely-promised enjoyments; just as if no testimony of its vanity existed in the experience of others, in the concurring verdict of their own consciences, in the word, or in the providence of God. ' O that men were wise; that they understood these things; that they would consider their latter end!' Remember, ye infatuated votaries of the world, the solemn hour is fast approaching, when you must have done with time, and all its passing concerns. That hour will infallibly awaken you, if you are not happily awakened earlier, to an appalling conviction of the truth which has now, and so often, been urged upon your timely consideration. The special hand of Death will then write, in dark but too legible characters, on every thing from which you have been seeking pour happiness, ' Vanity of van ities; vanity of vanities; ALL IS VANITY.'—O then, be wise in time. You are in quest of what never has been and never can be found from the sources to which you are repairing for it. The search for happiness amongst ' the things of this world,' has been, shall be, must be, a fruitless labor. It is the toil

> ' Of dropping buckets into empty wells,
> And growing old in drawing nothing up.'

" To you is the divine invitation addressed, and to all who are feeling the thirst of nature for satisfactory enjoyment:—' Ho, every one that thirsteth, come ye to the waters; and he that hath no money; come ye, buy and eat; yea come, buy wine and

milk, without money and without price   Where-
fore do ye spend money for that which satisfieth
not ?   Hearken diligently unto me, and eat ye that
which is good, and let your soul delight itself in
fatness.   Incline your ear, and come unto me :
hear, and your soul shall live.'   This expostulation
addressed to you by the God of heaven in infinite
condescension and kindness, is recommended to
your attention and obedience by the impressive appeal of the Saviour of sinful men ;—' For, what is
a man profited, if he shall gain the whole world,
and lose his own soul ?   For the Son of Man shall
come in the glory of his Father, and with his an
gels ; and then shall he reward every man accord
ing to his works.'   ' What profit' shall a man
then have, ' of all his labor which he hath taken un
der the sun ?'   The favor of God ;—the love of
Christ ;—the blessing of Heaven, mingling with
all the good and evil of life, enhancing the one,
and sweetening and sanctifying the other ; the ' ex
ceeding great and precious promises' of ' the life
that now is, and of that which is to come,'—the
faith of which inspires • the peace which passeth
all understanding ;'—the spiritual joy of ' fellowship with the Father, and his Son Jesus Christ,'
and with the children of God, the excellent of the
earth ;—and the blessed hope of eternal life,—of
glory and honor, and immortality :—these are sources of felicity. worthy of your rational and immortal natures. pure and dignified, substantial and everlasting.   Believe in the Lord Jesus Christ ; come
to God in his name ;—accept the mercy offered,
through his mediation, in the Gospel ; and all these
blessings, in time and eternity shall be yours
Wardlaw on Ecclesiastes.